WHITE SUNSET

Book 5: Gods & Assassins

Frank Kennedy

Dedicated to everyone who doesn't know how to call it quits

A note from the author:

Please read the first four books of *Gods & Assassins* before you begin this tale. I'd love for you to become part of my literary family. Sign up for my newsletter, which drops every three weeks along with free books and special offers. You can also follow me on Facebook, where you'll find me hanging out daily. Come on over and let's chat!

1

Collectorate Standard Year (SY) 5390

GODS WEREN'T SUPPOSED TO DREAM. What'd be the point? If you could travel anywhere in an instant, control life and death, witness the history of the universes from A to Z, experience the Dawn of the Great Fire and marvel at the Vanishing of the Final Light, what's left to imagine?

Moon and I hadn't dreamed in two thousand years. That was the price for leaving our human bodies. Our consciousness merged with a syneth core. We felt lighter without the baggage of an organic brain.

We agreed: Dreams had existed solely to torture us from birth. They told young Moon to embrace his inner lunatic and kill his family. He hid the urges but barely. Me? I lived on a planet where I didn't belong with a family that begged for an excuse to toss me aside.

Yeah. Bedtime was a nightmare waiting in the wings.

I'd wake in a sweat, my pulse racing the 100-meter dash. The worse bit was trying to analyze what the images meant. Some folks said dreams were symbolic, others claimed they were prophetic, while the most rational insisted they were simply the subconscious trying to make sense of the universe.

Naturally, I never listened to the rational folks. That got me into more than a little trouble. So I was not pleased ten minutes ago – furious, actually – when I closed my eyes for a moment, only to be assaulted by a dream. Or something to that effect.

I had planned to meditate on the future of Black Star's inevitable transition from Desperido. Over the past five weeks, violence between the cartels increased; the anti-Collectorate movement made martyrs of nine protestors we assassinated at Conquillos Base; and most of our forces remained off world to protect our Motif facilities.

Then there was Ixoca. He teased us for weeks about an imminent gathering of his Children of Orpheus. 'White Sunset,' he called it. Yet he offered no timeline, no instructions. I couldn't act against him until he opened the perfect door.

I had my suspicions, of course. Yet none of his Children gave away the secret, no matter how closely I looked through their many eyes. They were a cagey lot on a good day.

Perspective. That's all I needed. A few minutes alone in the dark to assess and find perspective. Instead, along came a dream.

A vision. A message. A prophecy. A shadow from an earlier life. Whatever. Like most dreams, it made little sense.

I walked through a dark corridor inside an asteroid called The Hold. That much I recognized. It was my home for a short time and the place where my reign of omnipotence ended. Yet I felt cold, and the air was moist — a far cry from the reality.

I ventured into a large kitchen, where soldiers inexplicably cooked a bounty from the sea. They taunted me, which made sense given that they were the enemy. They wore the turtle green body armor of Swarm F-grounders and a scorpion tattoo at the base of their right cheek.

They had no business at The Hold. They lost the war; Moon and I made damn sure of it. Yet they behaved like they belonged, as if they lived there for generations.

Huh.

I took a seat at a long table and waited to be served. Naturally, they ignored me. Then someone reached over my shoulder with a foot-long serrated blade. Rather than slice my throat, the owner buried his knife into the steel table. Sparks flew.

He dragged that knife through the steel as if it was cardboard. Flames rose in its path, but they didn't bother this fella. He twisted and curved that blade through a raging fire.

He yanked the blade away, leaving nothing but embers and a

sunrise-orange outline. At first glance, it was either an S or a reptile. Upon closer inspection, three horizontal lines extended inward from the upper curve. A pyramid grew from the base of the lower curve.

Before I contemplated its significance, an F-grounder tossed me a plate of raw fish, which landed above the carving.

The asshole mocked me.

That's where the dream ended. I didn't appreciate being mocked in any context, and I damn sure wasn't about to stand for it. I opened my eyes and summoned the malgado within me.

"Ixoca, is this your handiwork?"

The Jewel hesitated to respond – standard operating procedure in recent weeks.

"What seems to be your concern, Royal?"

"I had a dream. Tell me this is not a new feature."

He pixelated red.

"Unlike my Children, I cannot access your consciousness. However, if you told me what you saw, I might proffer an analysis."

"I'm sure you would. You've spent a thousand years entering your Children's dreams. Seen it all, I suspect."

Ixoca grinned, a rare expression of emotion.

"It has better helped me to understand the human construct."

"Not to mention allowing for some healthy back-door manipulation."

"That, too. Anything else, Royal?"

"Other than an answer to the question Moon and I have been asking for months? No."

Before the Jewel faded, he added:

"A few more days, Royal. Then you will know everything."

"I'd ask you to promise, but I'm sure you'll hedge."

"Ah. You've come to know me too well. In this case, I *will* promise. The final preparations have been made. The invitations accepted. Travel arrangements secured."

OK, so that last bit was new. Maybe if I pushed for more intel ...

"Ixoca, I realize this event is the culmination of your quest. But I do have practical concerns. As you've noticed, we continue to send more fighters and contractors off world. Desperido will soon become redundant. How many Black Star fighters will you require?"

He surprised me with an instant response.

"Sixty to seventy will suffice. Your current roster in Desperido is one hundred twenty. I will not stretch your resources unfairly."

"Good to know, my friend."

Why not tell me sooner? Was he testing me? Did he fear I'd shove the whole damn operation off Azteca to keep my folks beyond his reach? The thought crossed my mind.

Yeah, no. Too soon to spark his paranoia. I needed him blind to what Moon and I had in store. As long as he didn't know about Theo and Addis, victory remained plausible.

"Anything else, Royal?"

"Nothing for now. I'm sure you're a busy Jewel these days."

He vanished, but Ixoca never truly disappeared. He maintained a constant eye on his favorite fallen gods.

The buzzkill of my first dream in two millennia diminished the allure of quiet time. I linked into my partner's mind. Moon was inside Desperido Control briefing the next commander of our Inuit facility.

"Cut it short, my friend. We need to talk."

"I wanted this over ten minutes ago, partner. See you outside."

Shortly after the merge, Moon and I assumed our internal dialogue would be shielded from the Jewel's ears. We thought wrong. Our megalomaniacal ally was both busybody and know-it-all but never spoke in a harsh or condescending tone.

Yet.

Moon approached me outside our little home with an expression more dour than usual. He tried to hide aggravation behind his unruly beard. I assumed the latest of many briefings rubbed him raw.

"Concerns, my friend?"

"Not what you think, Royal."

"Then everything's good with Inuit?"

Moon nodded.

"Kato's a fine leader. He'll keep the workers in line."

"What's the concern?"

Typically, Moon spoke his mind without care for the immediate effect. He only checked himself when worried about Ixoca.

"I'm not sure, partner. I ... I think it's all getting ahead of us."

"No one suggested forming an empire was simple. But I take your point. We're maxing our resources."

In addition to posting sixty percent of our army at the four off-world facilities, twenty percent of our civilians had joined the interstellar operation. We sent teams of both to strike deals for new smuggling routes, scout locations on additional planets, purchase new transports, and refine Motif packages to include more commodities. Desperido's population leveled off to how we found it seven months ago.

"I don't mind dipping my hand into business, Royal. I can stomach this tedious shit because I know what we're building."

"And because you know the next slaughter is never far off."

Moon graced me with a smile.

"It helps."

"You're not hard to read, my friend. But something else is troubling you. Still uneasy about Riyadh?"

He grunted like a surly old man.

"I don't agree with your decision. For all we know, turning down that job will change the timeline."

"I'm certain that's where the Prez will die. If we kill the asshole who's planning her assassination ..."

"We have no proof he's the one."

Two weeks ago, Bart detected the beacon *Symphony New World*. I flew to 40-Cignus, made certain Leonard had not laid a trap, and retrieved a memglass from the drop. This time, however, I analyzed the job, copied the data, and returned the memglass to the casement. As far as Leonard knew, we weren't interested.

He spoke to the President a week later with Chief of Staff Kai Parke present. I watched as he voiced that very concern. They wanted us to kill Ahmed Faez, head of the Emir's Royal Guard, and make it look like an inside job. They believed Faez would shift the Emir's position to one bent toward independence. Riyadh almost broke away shortly after the People's Collectorate formed. President Aleksanyan thought they'd try again under Faez's influence.

"If our friends won't act," she said, "we need to get the job done ourselves. Do we have any SI contacts on the inside?"

"No," Leonard said. "They're buttoned up tight."

"Then we have no choice. I need a face to face with the Emir. If I don't counter Faez and his extremists, we'll lose Riyadh."

Despite Leonard's objections, the Prez ordered Kai to accelerate plans for a state visit. The timeline said it would be her last. If we took out Faez, she might never visit.

I made the proper decision. Moon thought we faced something more complex than a binary choice. He might've been right. I monitored Riyadh's deepstream news daily.

"All options remain on the table, my friend. We may yet have reason to intervene. But there's another matter I need to discuss. Why I pulled you from the meeting."

"Not another administrative headache?"

"No. I experienced something worrisome a short while ago. I find it hard to admit … never saw it coming. Moon, I had a dream."

His eyes glazed over. Did he not see the problem?

"Oh. Another one of your grand revelations?"

"No. A *dream*. As in, something we're incapable of. Worse, it was a waking dream."

Moon shrugged. Not the response I expected.

"Sounds like a psychotic break or a glitch in the syneth core. Happened to me all the time when I was insane."

"Those were hallucinations. I was there. I restrained you daily. This, my friend, was a dream. A trip into another reality. Incoherent but potentially laced with symbols. The art of a subconscious I no longer possess."

He mustered a passive frown.

"Did you speak to Ixoca?"

"He said it's not him or a function of the merger."

"It has to be connected. Nothing else makes sense."

"I'm surprised you'd say that after all we've seen."

Moon studied me with quizzical eyes, like I were a stranger.

"Tell me your dream."

I guided him through but left out the description of the carving. If the symbol meant something of value, sharing with Ixoca posed a potential danger.

Moon looked away. He studied central avenue, where tables were being set up for the evening's main event.

"A dream," he said, expressionless. "Why now, you think?"

"I've barely had time to theorize. It's possible you're right. A psychotic glitch in the syneth. Could be a one-off."

He muttered. "Yeah. Maybe."

"You sound skeptical, my friend."

He reached inside his jacket for a cigar.

"I didn't say anything at first because I've been there."

"Moon, what are you talking about?"

He held the cigar shy of his lips. I heard a confession coming.

"It happened this morning. I wrote it off as another glitch. I never thought it might be a dream."

OK, this day just got a whole lot more interesting.

"Tell me, Moon."

"It was brief. Maybe fifteen seconds. I saw myself in my father's lab. It was before I met you. Father wasn't there."

"Who was?"

"Swarm. High ranking officers. They huddled around a device that fired a laser at something ... I couldn't see through them. There was fire. And it was done."

I didn't believe in coincidence, but I believed in Moon. I leaned toward a theory I proposed long before we met the Jewel. If I was right, this moment required some verbal gymnastics. Time to put on a show for our so-called ally.

"I'd say the timing all but seals it, my friend. It must be the merger, Ixoca's protest notwithstanding. This is clearly a sign of a shift in our matrix. It's tapping into our memories and twisting them. It's logical we'd experience the effect within a few hours of each other. I suspect our syneth is evolving. Perhaps even developing a type of subconscious. Nothing we should worry over."

Moon lit the cigar and contemplated my cover story. After a puff or two, he nodded.

"Hope you're right. I don't have time to go insane again."

I chuckled. "It does tend to hurt efficiency. You know who would've excelled in a moment like this? Theo and Addis. They offered solutions to every problem. Of course, half the time they spouted whatever nonsense came to mind."

Did Moon follow my coded language?

"Yes, partner. They knew how to set us straight when we didn't know where to turn."

Good. He followed.

"I would go so far as to say that if Theo were here now, he'd suggest my memories were speaking to me. He'd analyze every part of my dream and develop the most nonsensical, totally illogical, but remarkably pleasing interpretation."

"Agreed. Addis would do the same for me."

Our *D'ru-shayas* dared not respond, of course. They knew how to listen while remaining hidden from Ixoca and examine the inner workings of our syneth matrix. If these dreams arose from the place where I suspected, Theo and Addis would unlock the truth.

In time to make a difference? That was another issue.

Earlier, Moon asked, "Why now?" I had an inkling, so I pushed our coded repartee to another level.

"Being back in your father's lab must have been awkward. You spent much of your childhood helping him with experiments."

Moon shook his head.

"I never think about the years before you came along."

"Understandable. But it must have rekindled thoughts about both your father and mother. Yes?"

His demeanor shifted a touch. Did he get my meaning? I tried to avoid direct eye contact; no point in providing Ixoca with visual cues.

"Father and Mother weren't important to me after I left Hokkaido. I don't care to revisit those years, Royal."

"Of course, my friend. Difficult times. Painful. Father and Mother kicked my ass out of the house and never spoke to me again. I used to wonder if they thought about me."

Moon walked away in a cloud of smoke.

"You'll decipher it. I have things to do."

Yep. He got my meaning. I'm not sure Moon believed my theory, but I doubted Ixoca found the exchange intriguing enough to linger on it. Our minor linguistic victory would have to suffice for now.

Gods did not dream. Today changed nothing.

My surreal trip inside the asteroid wasn't a dream at all.

It was a message.

Father and Mother, the old bastard who reigned since the Dawn of Creation and cast us down into the Fort of Inarra, hadn't forsaken Its defeated gods.

I long suspected It planted us here with the future in mind. Moon had refused to believe when I said *Father and Mother* knew we'd come into contact with a Jewel of Eternity.

Shit.

Of course It had a plan. Doesn't every omnipotent asshole?

We were Its tools, but to do what precisely?

The thought of what lay ahead buoyed my spirits. I awaited the next message with excitement.

Naturally, the thrill did not survive the evening's disaster.

2

DESPERIDANS CAME A LONG WAY in seven months. These former mole people discovered the joy of celebrating each other's success in the light. They relearned social graces, partied until late hours, and appeared fit for proper society. In other words, their town was doomed.

I doubted most would leave here with regret. Sizeable bank accounts offered everyone a fresh start, whether on Azteca or another world with a Black Star imprint.

These people weren't stupid: Desperido was a boomtown, the kind that inevitably went bust. They'd soon leave behind nothing but red dust and memories. Humans loved their nostalgia.

Moon, Saul, and I discussed how it would end. We intended to depart last. Mr. Mayor would have the honor of setting off the explosives. We'd watch from a safe distance inside Bart.

That was the vision. Very tidy.

Of course, it wouldn't be so simple. Our growing list of enemies were as likely to finish the job and sooner.

That concern plus a message from the single most powerful entity in all of recorded time weighed heavily as I joined our evening party on central avenue. Not that I allowed anyone to notice. Why spoil their great fun? Tonight's party was special.

Saul greeted me with a firm handshake and a cordial smile. We saw each other daily when I wasn't mission-bound, yet he always behaved as if it were the first time. He took to his role as a one-term politician. The phrase I was looking for? Glad-hander.

That title often carried a negative connotation, pointing to a lack of sincerity. It certainly described me on countless occasions, but never Saul. He had evolved beyond master forger into a reputable man who no longer hid behind a mask. I found him fascinating and a true outlier.

"It's a wonderful turnout," Saul said amid the laughter and music. "I hope our man of the hour appreciates it."

"I'd call even odds at this point."

Saul laughed. "Such a cynic, Raul."

"You mean to say, 'not naïve.'"

He sipped on a dark ale, his favored beverage.

"*Cynic.* Literally. When was the last time you trusted a human?"

"I trust everyone, Saul. I trust them to behave foolishly, selfishly, recklessly, and treacherously. Thus, I'm prepared to respond in kind."

"There you are! *Cynic.*"

I played along. This little game lifted my spirits.

"As you wish. What odds would you assign?"

"Oh, I'd have to go at least sixty-forty in favor."

"Hedging your bet, I see."

Saul nodded toward Ship, who approached from Mod 3.

"He bears no resemblance to the boy who used to serve this ale. I once pitied him."

"And now?"

"To be frank, Raul, he frightens me."

"Why? You consider him a threat?"

Saul lowered his voice and leaned in.

"He poses no danger to us. But outsiders? Our enemies? He'll show no mercy."

Saul didn't mean it as a compliment, but I took it as one. The kid had grown five inches since we met. His mustache thickened, his shoulders broadened, and his swagger deepened. Appearance alone demanded greater respect. Yet I focused on what he carried inside: A steel spine and a frozen heart.

His revenge tour on Everdeen did not destroy him, as I feared in the days afterward. I watched through his eyes while veterans who lost their way after the war encouraged Ship to choose between the man he wanted to be and the one he was becoming. I'll admit: They were better teachers. He could only learn so much from a god.

Now, he was cut sharp as a knife beneath a shaved scalp. His probing eyes showed no fear. He carried himself with the edge of a soldier and the aura of a stone cold killer. If Ship survived our exodus from this planet, he'd become the enforcer I envisioned from the early days.

If.

He arrived at the party along with two vets in their forties but did not come directly over to me, as he might have in the past. Rather, he acknowledged me and Saul with a curt nod. I saw "Boss" fall off his lips, then he made a straight line toward the food.

"I wonder whether he was warned," Saul said.

"Not in any conversation I watched. I filtered out most of his interactions. Ship spends the bulk of his free time alone. Exercise by day and pom-reading by night."

"What does he read?"

"Military history. Weapons design. Analysis of the criminal mind."

Saul shadowed his eyes, but he couldn't hide the disappointment.

"You must be pleased."

"I am, Saul. The day he led me on a tour of this town, I made off-handed promises to win his favor. Never thought about actually keeping them until sometime later."

"He'll hold you to them now."

Saul and I split up to mingle, as had become tradition in the short history of these communal affairs. We agreed to meet back at the podium in ten minutes to give our welcome speeches. At present, an eclectic band of veterans and older contractors occupied the small stage, playing traditional Aztecan folk music. Their chaotic performance showed passion but a decided lack of practice. I turned down my audio sensors to filter out the cacophony.

Music never mattered much in my lives, but it uplifted the humans in my midst. So who was I to argue with its power?

Genoa, a day returned from her stint on G'hladi, sauntered alongside. She had washed away her rainbow crew cut and settled for jet black after taking a command role.

"Mind if I have a word, boss?"

"Always."

She carried a small plate of baked goods.

"Care for one? They're damn good."

"I'll pass, my friend. I can guess what's on your mind."

Genoa bit into a creamy bar and said:

"That obvious? Raul, I'm happy you and Stopper had confidence in me to run security for the Rahmati Plantation. But ..."

"It's boring you senseless. Correct?"

"I wouldn't say boring. More like ... quiet. It's an easy ride. I joined the militia for action. I'm best with a gun in my hand, not planning a duty rotation."

I peeked in on Genoa from time to time; the G'hladi facility ran at high efficiency, easily our most stable off-world venture. She already voiced her concerns to Bett upon return.

"You want an assignment with danger. Yes?"

"I do."

"Your bank account is overflowing. Haven't you earned the chance to enjoy your newfound good fortune? There are many palatial homes in that region, long abandoned. You should claim one."

My proposal elicited a mocking laugh.

"And do what? Invite the neighbors over for cookouts?"

"Humans have long enjoyed that sort of thing. Look around."

"It's not me, boss. I was thinking about Bolivar. We don't have the mountain tribes under control, and we're on our third commander."

"I see. You want to replace Inky Sisal?"

"Not replace. Join. He needs a tactical advisor who will take on the dirty work. I was there when we destroyed the Pezos cartel."

13

She was a go-getter, no doubt. Fueled by adrenaline, willing to run into fire if need be. Black Star had dozens like her, but we needed to spread them around.

"You're not wrong about Bolivar, but Stopper and I agree: We need you on G'hladi for now." Her shoulders sagged. "Understand this: We're entering the most dangerous phase of our growth. Certain events will soon transpire on Azteca. They'll determine the shape of our future. If they go badly for us here, our off-world holdings must remain stable. After we're done with this planet, we'll revisit your role."

Genoa smiled in resignation.

"Promise, boss?"

"You don't need to ask, my friend. You belong to the table of trust. That will never change."

She finished off the cream bar.

"Gotcha. Oh, and you really should try these. Very good."

In many ways, that exchange summed up my life. On the one hand, I plotted the future of an interstellar criminal empire; on the other, I massaged and cajoled to keep everyone content.

Cream bars. Native music. A neighborhood block party.

Very human.

Eh.

I sought out Moon and Saul then retreated to the stage, where I waited for the band to finish its last off-key melody. I sent them away with exaggerated praise. Per our script, Saul grabbed the crowd's attention – I estimated about five hundred had poured out of the bunkers and modules. They settled quickly.

"Good evening, Desperido," Saul began, raising his glass of ale. "Good evening, Black Star." After a few whoops and hollers, "I'm so heartened by the turnout. I'm astounded by what we've done in seven months. My only regret is that hundreds of our dear comrades cannot be with us. But their absence speaks to our remarkable success. I offer a toast to every member of Black Star scattered across other systems. To our comrades and to the future!"

Glasses, pitchers, and bottles lifted toward the stars, which crept out from behind the sun's dying light. Rather than compete with the cheers, I popped into Saul's mind.

"Well said, my friend. You lift them up; I temper their hopes. A nice one-two combination."

"Only for you, boss."

I stepped before the microphone and tipped my hat, which I wore with considerable panache. I'd miss it after we left this dreadful world.

My speech began with a tone at its most dulcet.

"After that fine opening, to which I can't hope to match, I will try to keep my thoughts brief. First, an update. The next dividends will appear in your bank accounts five days hence. You'll be pleasantly surprised by the increase."

A rising tide of applause echoed into the desert until it turned thunderous. I slipped Saul a devilish side-eye.

"Apparently, I *can* match," I said inside his mind.

"Never doubted, Raul."

When the crowd settled, I continued.

"Before we resume the festivities, I wish to pass along two substantial pieces of news. First, the facility at Ennoi on Indonesia Prime will begin running at full capacity in one week. Behind projections, yes, but we believe its strategic position will provide us the greatest profit potential of our four locations. This means we will be posting more teams of soldiers and contractors to that region.

"The planet sits at a nexus for the night market. Five worlds within fifteen light-years of each other. Our next major expansion will focus on the entire Perseus Cluster. Once we secure that sector, we'll have solid routes to everywhere except Aeterna."

I paused a beat. Dare I give away too much? Hmm. No. I hadn't yet divulged those plans even to Moon.

"The immortals pose a different challenge. We'll save them for last. Here's the upshot, my friends. Our lovely little oasis on the Naugista Plateau will soon outlive its usefulness. We've all seen this

15

coming, though no one wished to admit it. Our future lies elsewhere. Therefore, many of you face difficult choices.

"In the coming days, long-term residents will receive a digiform. You will state your intention. Three choices: Leave Desperido for another home on Azteca; join Black Star's off-world operations; or take your wealth to the stars and settle on another world as a private citizen. You did not sign a pact with Black Star, so we will not oblige you to follow us.

"I can't say how long we'll occupy Desperido, only that her many years of service will not go unnoticed or unrewarded at the end."

Ixoca heard every word; I intended the speech as much for him as the residents. Perhaps I provided a sense of urgency.

"I don't wish to dim your joy. Rather, I hope you'll appreciate what brought us here tonight, and that this might be the last time we celebrate in grand spirits. So, to that end, let's continue the festivities. Mr. Mayor?"

Saul regained the microphone.

"Tonight holds special meaning, for we honor someone who arrived in Desperido six years ago, who we all came to know, and who has grown from civilian into soldier, from boy to man."

Many eyes turned to Ship, who showed no evidence of joy, though I suspected the shock had waylaid him.

"Ship Foster, congratulations on turning seventeen."

Wild cheers, shoulder pats, handshakes, and spilled liquor ensued. Calls for him to say a few words, which must've been his worst nightmare, appeared to freeze the kid in place.

I jumped inside his mind.

"You're respected and loved, my friend. They'll understand if you hold your tongue."

Even in the dim light, water glistened in his eyes.

"It's not my birthday yet," Ship replied.

"Not on the Collectorate Standard Calendar. But I researched your local birthdate. Based on system calculations and time differential, you turned seventeen shortly before noon. We wanted to throw you a party today, not two weeks from now. Smile, Ship."

He did, albeit forced.

I replaced Saul at the microphone.

"Ship was among the first residents I met. Most of you don't know the integral role he played in bringing us here. Thank you, my friend."

I bowed. Well, more like tipped forward slightly. The day I bowed to a human would certainly be my last.

"Many worlds have a song for occasions such as this. I've never heard it myself. Apparently you Aztecans know it well. Mr. Mayor?"

Saul led a loud, boisterous chorus in the singing of a tone-deaf little ditty called "Birthday Salutations." It was more horrifying than the band, although Ship's expression said he felt a deeper agony. Still, he took a breath and sighed when it was over.

He raised his hands and muttered a response.

"Thank you, everyone."

Few in the crowd heard him, but humans believed it was the thought that counted. Good enough.

"The positive vibes continue, my friends. My partner Ilan has a special present for the town."

Moon dreaded this moment; naturally, I relished it.

Saul looked behind the stage toward the egress to Mod 1 and nodded my way. Our surprise waited in the wing.

Moon cleared his throat into the microphone and shuffled his feet as the crowd silenced. My best friend proved the old sentiment that public speaking could humble anyone, even the most ruthless killing machine I'd ever known.

"The ... the man responsible ..." He shot me an icy cold side-eye and reset. I never wished my partner harm, of course, but my joy knew no bounds. I'd mock him about this moment for the next few centuries.

"Leaders command the stage," I told him earlier. "You can't hide forever, my friend."

Moon recovered before the moment turned embarrassing.

17

"The reason we're here today started long before Raul and I came to Desperido. The man responsible for our wealth and influence created a product that will be worth billions of credits very soon." Moon looked over my shoulder toward the module. "Everyone, welcome back the master of Motif. A man of courage and vision (that bit was mine). Elian!"

The applause for Ship paled to the rapturous ovation for our resident drug lord, who should have fallen at Indonesia Prime five weeks ago but defied ridiculous odds.

Elian raised his fists like a fighter entering the ring and blew past his entourage. The new left leg worked in perfect sync with his right after a few days of glitches. Even syneth integrations proved dicey on occasion.

He bounded onto the stage, no less the showman than the last time he graced a central avenue celebration. Neither he nor the adoring crowd seemed the slightest bit hesitant about Elian's stark facial contrast.

He lost most of the right side to shrapnel; it should have killed him on the spot. The surgeon's work and continued reconstruction with phasic holotools restored most of what was destroyed. Wisely, he turned down my offer of a syneth patch that might recapture his original beauty. I offered no guarantees it would work after interfacing with his brain. He agreed to a slimmer alternative.

A syneth glove as soft as human skin but much stronger covered the grotesque scars and the hole once occupied by an eye. The tone did not match Elian's natural color, a difference only noticeable up close. His right nostril was slightly smaller than the left, and his lips crimped at the right edge.

Elian and his fire-red, intricately coiffed hair commanded the scene. He wore his trademark black trench coat and a jewel studded to each ear. To no surprise, his walk with death had done little to humble the man.

"My people, I have returned!"

His proclamation drew another round of cheers. Though most of

18

Desperido visited during his rehabilitation, many were stunned to see him arrive with such vigor. His back proved the biggest obstacle to recovery. It had suffered far more damage than first thought. Publicly, we downplayed his timetable. Tonight's appearance was Elian's idea.

He belonged on a stage.

"Thank you, Ilan. Those words meant everything to me."

Moon cracked an awkward grin and clearly wanted off the stage. Elian wouldn't stand for it.

"If it wasn't for you and my dear friend Raul, I wouldn't be here today." He faced the crowd. "It's a hell of thing working for gods, ain't it? What would they say if you went back to your hometowns and told people, 'Guess who I work for?' They'd reckon you were batshit." He allowed the laughter and whoops to settle. "Here's what I know. I got two healthy legs, I can stand upright, and I can count from one to ten. That's a miracle.

"Oh, and nobody worry: You won't hear about me on a battlefield again. I'll leave that job to the true professionals." He pointed to men and women in camouflage. "To Black Star!"

The crowd responded in kind.

"So, that's all I have to say. Except this. I can't remember the last time I had a good whiskey or smoked a fine cigar. Time to make that right, my people. Thank you all!"

There he was, unabashed and returned to his old form, though I knew Elian must have been in considerable pain. Some nerve issues in his back had not been resolved.

He hugged us and made merry with his devotees. He'd absorb their adulation and soon forget about the folly that almost killed him. Such was the life of a narcissist. Even one with half a lovely face.

Tonight, however, his joy did not last long.

3

IN RETROSPECT, I SHOULD HAVE SEEN it coming. Our desert home flourished too long without disruption. We piled up victories with minimal loss of life. Profits exceeded our projections tenfold. Moon and I gave form to a dream, but it was all too easy. Fate loved to wield its odious hand at the moment we least expected.

I stood in a billowing cloud of smoke as the original table of trust reunited for the first time in two months. Elian relished his first cigar, a fat, black bastard that trumped Moon's usual. Ship sucked on a smaller variety, no bigger than an index finger. Genoa preferred a cheroot in a brown wrap. Saul loathed cigars, so he passed. To his credit, however, he endured without objection.

"Never thought I'd live to see the day," Elian said between puffs. "When Ilan hauled me out of the jungle, I knew I was done for."

Moon grunted. "It wasn't your time."

Elian studied Moon with an air of suspicion.

"You really believe that?"

"Some people have destinies. Yes."

The answer shocked me. Moon spoke from personal experience, but I never heard him talk of human fate in those terms. The first time I claimed our presence on Azteca was meant to be, Moon dismissed me. What changed his mind? It had to be more than our merger with Ixoca.

"Then my destiny must be special," Elian replied. "Can't see why else the universe would hold onto an asshole like me."

"Perhaps," Saul countered, "it has an impaired sense of humor."

"Good one, Mayor."

Elian offered Saul a fresh cigar, which he refused for the second time. Elian shoved it in Saul's shirt pocket anyway.

"Expand your range of simple pleasures, Saul."

Saul smelled the tobacco and sighed.

"I'll take the suggestion under advisement."

Elian gigged Ship, who smoked in relative silence since we huddled amid the masses.

"Hey, limb buddy. Congrats on the seventeenth."

Ship didn't break a smile; rather, he fixated on Elian's hair.

"What's with the red?"

"Wuh? You don't like?"

The kid shrugged. "You remind me of a jester."

"What's that?"

"A clown."

"Ya think?"

Ship peeled his eyes away and shrugged. Those two became close in the early months of my regime, but I sensed a gap as Elian's fame and ego diminished all those around him. I suppose Moon felt the same about me when I reveled in our takeover of this town.

Genoa intervened before a spat erupted.

"I'm the queen of color. Some fit, some don't. Tried a rainbow for a while. It's good to experiment. That's what life's for."

She and Elian tapped glasses. Ship wanted none of it.

"Soldiers don't have the luxury to experiment. We follow orders or we die."

Glum, albeit true. Not the sort of banter for this occasion. Saul recognized and stepped in.

"Ship, you're correct about a soldier. You chose to shave your head. You made a statement befitting your role as you see it. Elian has done the same. Both choices are valid and worthy of respect."

Ship nodded in that noncommittal way teens did, often followed by mutterings that included "whatever."

"Yeah. Sorry, Elian. I didn't mean nothing."

"No worries, limb buddy."

"Please don't call me that. It's weird."

"We're long past that, my friend. Tell him, boss. We're the only humans walking around with syneth prosthetics."

Whenever Elian opened his mouth, he had to make certain the neighbors heard. Not wise.

"You are," I said. "But I recall us having a conversation about the need for secrecy. The wrong people will kill you for what you're wearing. They'll take those limbs and conduct experiments. You do not want a future where the human race mass-produces syneth. Trust me on this one."

Moon disagreed with replacing Ship's metal arm for that very reason. However, he never voiced an objection when Elian stood to benefit. By then, Moon lost his objectivity regarding humans. So had I. It would likely be our undoing.

"Shit, boss. Sorry. Reckon I was having too much fun."

Neither recipient knew the whole truth about their limbs: I installed a failsafe. In the event of death, Ship's arm and Elian's leg would incinerate. Same would happen if the limbs were forcibly removed from their live bodies.

A damned fool, I was not.

"Forgiven, my friend. You're celebrating a second lease. In fact, why don't you spread your considerable wings among the crowd. Conduct a survey about the red hair. Yes?"

"Gotcha, Raul."

Elian excused himself to Ship's obvious pleasure. Or so I detected from the rolled eyes.

"He's living his best life," I told the kid. "He'll find his way back to solid ground soon enough. What about you? I hope you hold no grudges for the birthday surprise."

22

"No, boss. Yeah, it was nice. To be honest, I wasn't in the mood for a party tonight. My mates dragged me out here."

"They had their orders."

Ship cracked a smile. Progress.

"I wondered why they wouldn't take no for an answer."

"Your birthday is a milestone, my friend. The future I promised is coming to pass. If you're to be one of our top enforcers, moments like this deserve to be recognized. *You* must be acknowledged, Ship. The others must be reminded of your standing in Black Star."

He perked his chin up.

"Appreciate it, boss. If you don't mind, I'd like to grab something to eat. Maybe there's still some cake."

Someone (I forgot who) decided birthdays included cake. I never heard of it growing up human on Hokkaido. We ate fish rolls, no different than most days.

Ship didn't wait for permission to leave. He pushed through the crowd toward the buffet.

Moon spoke his mind.

"I don't trust that kid anymore."

"Why in ten hells would you say that, my friend?"

Moon rolled the cigar between his teeth.

"He's not comfortable around us. It's been easy to see."

"Why, you think?"

"Come on, partner. You don't need an algorithm."

Saul stepped between us.

"Ilan's right. Ship is quantifiably a different person than the one you met seven months ago. Raul, he served drinks in a bar. Now, you ask him to kill on demand. The life you promised will be soaked in other men's blood. He sees himself becoming like the two of you, and a part of him is resisting."

As usual, Mayor Saul illuminated the moment.

"Of course, you're spot-on. But it's too late. The last piece of Ship's conscience is little more than a rabble-rouser. Every time he acts at our behest, that tiny voice will dim."

"I pray you're wrong, Raul. You may have the luxury of living without a conscience, but we do not. Ilan, I'm sure he's trustworthy. Employ patience. He'll adjust."

Saul excused himself, and Genoa soon after.

"I'll be back on G'hladi this time tomorrow," she said. "I'd like to see some of my old friends before I go."

I led Moon away from the crowd and continued the discussion inside our minds.

"Do you agree with Saul, my friend?"

"He doesn't understand our kind."

"True. He's not a killer. He might be the most principled human I've met in centuries. But he's not wrong. Your problem, Moon, is that you see yourself in Ship. You weren't cut out for this until I came into your life. The first time you killed was in self-defense. Even that, you struggled to overcome. Remember?"

"If you're talking about the Ajax ..."

"I am."

"I died soon after and woke up outside time itself. I had bigger concerns on my mind, Royal."

Fair point.

"Years later, after you became proficient in murder, you struggled to cross the line into full acceptance. Ship is going through a similar trial. In time, he'll take pride in every kill, as we do. Inflicting death and pain will become his day job."

Moon pulled on the last of his cigar and tossed it into the dust.

"Until he's killed."

"I can't see any other end. But they'll all die. Positions like his will become revolving doors. For Ship, it's a case of how soon. Months? Years? He'll give his life for Black Star. They all will. As Saul said: employ patience, my friend. Enjoy the progress we've ..."

Bett called my name. Her eyes moved front and center.

"Raul, Ilan. We have a problem. Incoming wormhole ..."

"Unauthorized?"

"Yes. Five seconds to aperture."

24

Bett contacted me from Desperido Control, which she volunteered to run while the duty officers took time away for the party. The wormhole tracker flickered on the holo in front of her. I didn't have enough time to see whether the flight originated on Azteca or in space.

"Moon, we've got troub ..."

I didn't know the half of it.

Wormhole apertures always excited me, going back to my first life. The sun flash arrived with a furious thunder created by a seal being broken on the black substrata beneath visible space. The swirl that followed offered adventure, a path to the unknown. It was a marvel created by *Father and Mother* long before mortals stood upright. A secret It allowed the lesser beings to discover in their own time.

Now some malgados were using it against Black Star.

When the aperture flashed open northeast of town, I did not marvel. Instead, I felt layers of trepidation. The aperture was too big and too close to make sense. It opened less than fifty meters from the outer edge of the oasis dome.

Someone on that ship screwed the pooch.

"What in ten hells?" Moon said.

A midsize transport emerged from the swirl, bearing down on Desperido at top speed. The ship was four times the size of our Scramjet Maria, decorated with missile launchers and forward turrets.

UNF? No. They wouldn't be this sloppy. They'd ...

The alarm sounded across Desperido, a critical klaxon for anyone still underground. Something was wrong; why hadn't our missiles activated sooner?

"Bett, fire everything we ..."

My order didn't matter. There wasn't time.

The transport fired its first missiles, but they impacted the oasis dome, which absorbed the energy. The crew must not have known how far our defenses extended. The cloak created a mirage by design.

The attacker smashed into the dome, which electrified in every damn direction. For a few seconds, night transitioned to dawn.

The transport's bow section burst into flames and disintegrated, shooting fiery projectiles toward us. The first ones hit the interior shield, which diminished their impact like an atmosphere acting on small meteors. Yet pieces got through.

The midship and engine array spun and splintered. Huge chunks blasted through both shields.

Where to run?

Fire rained on Desperido as if flung from a battery of trebuchets.

A chunk crashed within a few feet of the little home I shared with Moon. Much larger, spiraling ship segments spread a wide swathe of destruction.

Our people ran, ducked, and tried in vain to hide.

An explosion took out part of a module. Another chunk cratered on the western side of town, throwing up debris from bunker cubes beneath it.

As for the party crowd? Small pieces hit central avenue like a shower of laser bolts. Men fell.

Nothing compared to the largest shrapnel, which bore a wide hole through the cantina's only entrance.

And then it was over.

Parts of Desperido burned. Bodies lay about.

Seconds later, in shocked silence, our people rose to their feet.

"Find one alive," I told Moon, who raced into the center of chaos at top speed in search of enemy survivors. "Bett, announce Black Alert. I want our ships in the air."

"On it, Raul."

Her voice echoed across the citywide speakers. Our emergency defense plan designated small teams to remain on standby at a second's notice. All of them were likely on central avenue or inside the cantina when the debris hit. Yet I saw fighters race to our sedans and Scramjet when the order was given.

"Any sign of more incoming?"

"Negative, boss. We're clear for the moment."

"Where did that ship enter worm?"

"Definitely terrestrial. Retracing now."

"Advise when you have coordinates. What's the shield status?"

"Holding."

Now for the hard part. I hadn't been on the receiving end of an enemy attack since the Swarm war. Defeat had no place in our vocabulary. My thoughts turned to revenge, the last refuge of the furious and reckless.

Our people responded brilliantly. They put out fires, rushed to the wounded, and worked to rescue the trapped.

I entered the fray, passing many bodies en route. Yet I noticed most were not our people, and few lay contorted in one piece. They were charred, having fallen to the desert amid the firestorm.

"Who's responsible, Ixoca?"

This time, the Jewel did not hesitate.

"I'm accessing all my eyes, Royal, but no one seems to be aware of this attack."

"Ixoca, there are few entities with worm-capable ships of that class. Your Children control most of them. How do they know nothing?"

I carried on the dialogue with Ixoca while checking on the wounded. We'd have to prioritize them. Though we assembled a healthy medpod of phasic tools, it was not designed for mass injuries.

"Royal, if our influence blanketed the planet, I would not need to orchestrate an insurgency. We would simply take over without firing a shot. There are many in government, the regional constabularies, and even inside the shipping guilds who do not belong to me."

Eh. There was always a gap waiting to be seized upon.

"Who else?"

Ixoca pixelated red.

"The cartels. The Children of Orpheus have avoided their favor, with the exception of Vash Rodriguez. But you shut down the threat. Have you considered the interstellar night market? A competitor seeking to tear down Black Star and claim the Motif trade for itself?"

He sized up all but one remaining set of suspects.

"Whoever they are, they're amateurs. They didn't know the reach of our cloak shield. That would seem to rule out SI. Listen to me, Ixoca. I don't have time to see through the many eyes. I need you to talk to your generals. Be discreet. If those malgados aren't behind the attack, they know who to ask."

"My pleasure, Royal. I'll get on this at once. And my condolences for your losses tonight. Please, be with your people. They need you."

As the Jewel vanished, I hung on his final words.

Condolences. A human formality, often used by people who didn't actually care but felt obligated to acknowledge another's grief.

Huh. Had my paranoia kicked into high gear? Was the Jewel playing me?

Goddamn. If he was behind this somehow ...

But why? I saw no clear motive. He needed Black Star.

Unless ...

No. Too soon.

I'd have to consider that possibility tomorrow. For now, the ugly part of defeat reared itself around me.

I used my speed to carry badly wounded Desperidans to the medpod. I assisted the rescue effort outside the cantina, where most of the victims had fallen.

Too many thoughts at once. Back and forth with Bett, who oversaw the ongoing defense and determined the ship's origin. The coordinates made no sense and required further investigation.

"Bett, deepstream our off-world commanders. Tell them to raise their alert status."

"You think these fucks plan to hit us everywhere?"

"Doubtful, my friend. But without our shields, we would've lost the town. They need to reinforce defenses."

"On it, boss."

The next turning points happened seconds apart, tugging me in opposite directions.

Elian stumbled toward me, unharmed but stunned. The fiery

crashes must've taken him back to the Ularu Jungle on Indy Prime. The man with the biggest smile in Desperido cried from his one eye.

"Boss, y-you have to come."

I surged toward the cluster outside the cantina. Rescuers in camouflage passed me, holding up burned but breathing civilians. Genoa and Ship assisted, yet they both looked away when we made eye contact.

"Here, boss," Elian pointed. "Over here. I'm sorry. There weren't anything to be done for him."

My mind had been such a jumble, I filtered out most of Ixoca's many eyes to focus on Moon, Bett, and our security status. It didn't occur to me that among the dead …

Yet I should have known. A split second before I looked where Elian pointed, I realized whose eyes had vanished. Whose voice I had not heard since the aperture opened.

There wasn't much left of Saul.

He stared forever at the stars, blood splattered across his face and that scraggly gray beard. Nothing remained beneath his rib cage.

Other body parts laid about like a gruesome sculpture garden. Saul. Our people. The enemy. Amidst it all: The culprit.

The largest section of the crashed ship.

"I can't believe he's gone, boss. When do we fight back?"

When I led men into battle against the Swarm, I never learned the right things to say afterward. Grief and rage weren't as vital as preparing for the next inevitable slaughter.

Saul was a good goddamn human being. He knew what Moon and I were, yet he chose to stay. He chose to lead.

"Calm, Elian. Help others as best you can. We'll remember him when the time is right."

Oh, the goddess of timing. Three seconds later, Moon said:

"Found one alive. He's conscious."

"Keep him that way, my friend. I have questions."

4

ONE MAN DID NOT GO DOWN with his ship. The section that crashed into the eastern side of Mod 4 ejected a few bodies, but a poor sod had the good fortune to smack into the nearest undamaged portion of the roof and tumble over the edge. Moon found him trying without success to stand.

"Anything yet?" I asked upon arrival.

"No. He's groggy."

I pointed to the bloody mess erupting from his right eye.

"From the fall or your left hook?"

Moon sneered. "Both."

"Take care. He may be our only intel. Ixoca will talk to his generals, but he claims the Children of Orpheus are not to blame."

Moon almost overstepped.

"Ixoca claims many things. That doesn't mean ..."

I grabbed Moon by the shoulder and pushed him away from our favorite new prisoner.

"Settle, my friend. Use reason. Ixoca has no motive."

Actually, there might have been one, but saying it aloud was problematic on a good day. I'd seen this level of rage in Moon's eyes before; frankly, I was surprised he hadn't killed the enemy.

"Then who, Royal?"

"We'll find out and offer a speedy response. But now is not the time to lose our heads. Have you seen what we lost out there?"

"Through their eyes? No. I focused on finding these assholes."

He did a better job compartmentalizing than me.

"Saul's dead. I don't know how many more."

I saw a flicker of genuine concern.

"Saul? What about the command structure?"

"Most are with us still. Elian, Ship, Genoa – they're fine. Black Alert is working. Bett has it under control. We need to focus on this malgado. Not Ixoca or his people."

We'd have to deal with them someday soon. Our path intersected with theirs. Until then …

The prisoner groaned, so I bent my knees and guided him to a harsh new reality.

"Time to play ten questions, my friend."

"Wah?"

I saw nothing special in the young man, though he did seem somehow familiar. He was early twenties, with many tattoos on both arms, a nose ring, and slightly charred hair below his shoulders. He didn't wear a uniform but holstered two pistols which Moon acquired. The kid knew he was in a world of trouble when he opened those narrow, sepia eyes.

"Who … who are you? What h-happened?"

"Your ship crashed. Your crew is dead. By a stroke of remarkable fortune, you outlived them all."

He reached for his weapons instinctively but found nothing there.

"Let's start with a name."

His panicked eyes switched between Moon and I, but he reserved the greater terror for my partner. Understandable.

"No. No. I ain't to say nothing."

I flicked dust from his jeans and chuckled.

"Interesting. *I ain't to say nothing.* Does your response reflect your current confusion or general lack of education?"

"Wah? Please. I got nothing to say."

"I disagree, and so does my partner. When I ask a question, answer truthfully within five seconds, or Ilan will inflict horrifying pain. Trust me: He's quite brilliant at inducing agony without bringing on death."

Ah. His pants stained in the private area. Good.

"Question one: Your name is?"

He pushed the count to five before saying, "Armin. My name is Armin Salazar."

"Lovely start. Now, who do you work for?"

His eyes ballooned.

"No. No, please. They'll kill me."

"You misunderstand your predicament. Who do you work for?"

"Y-you'll kill me even if I talk."

He developed a defiant tone. Not brave, just foolish. That's when I heard something in his voice that brought me closer to the truth.

"Have we met before, Armin Salazar?"

Armin tightened his brow. The little cunt recognized *me*.

"No. But I heard about you." He leered at Moon. "And you."

Moon twisted his fingers into raw syneth and generated a foot-long steel corkscrew. Interesting choice. I grinned at my partner and then at Armin.

"I see the resemblance, my friend. You're Mando's child. Yes?"

"Mando?" Moon said. "The asshole from the first day?"

"The same, Ilan."

We met Mando and his sidekick Vincente shortly after arriving in Desperido to retrieve our armory. They finished off poor Esai and reached an understanding with me inside the cantina. Moon infected them with a terminal virus soon thereafter.

"Now, explain how you know about us and why you were aboard that ship."

Armin knew his life would soon end. Did he want to die button-lipped or as a squealer? I preferred the latter but assumed Moon would have to use him as a plaything first. Saul should have been here. He knew how to see through a human mask.

"You get nothing out of me."

Eh. Plaything, it was.

I entered Moon's mind.

"Take care, my friend. Make him hurt, but he must not pass out. We don't have the time."

"Can do, partner."

I gently slapped the poor sod.

"Each new day brings the hope of joy and the potential for pain. You have resigned yourself to the latter."

I wished him well and stepped away. Moon's left hand evolved into a drill. He positioned the corkscrew above Armin's shoulder and triggered the syneth device. It cut into the muscle and bone, sending the fool into a spasm of shrieks.

Meantime, I checked in through the many eyes of my lieutenants. Rescue operations continued at the cantina, as heavy tools removed the last impediment. Ship entered the cantina alongside Genoa. The place had likely served its final drinks.

Shouts for help; bodies crushed and/or buried beneath rubble; glass and wood fragments forming an ugly jungle; and a toxic smoke cloud. All amid dim lighting powered by the emergency generator.

I switched to Elian, who surveyed the western end of town, where a crater opened into the bunker cubes that once housed his nascent business. People underground called his name, begged for help. Most of his teams had transferred off world; they were the fortunate ones.

He froze as other contractors and a few fighters formed a chain to assist the rescue. I popped into his mind.

"Elian. Find your courage. You're not a soldier anymore. You must lead them."

"I ... I don't know how, boss."

"Be the man you were before Indonesia Prime but without the ego. Place them first, and they will follow. That's how Saul ran Desperido."

"I'll try."

"Do it or don't bother at all, my friend. This is no time for half-measures. You are still alive for a reason. Make it this. Understood?"

"Gotcha, boss."

I left Elian to fend for himself and returned to my pressing concern.

Armin's ripped jacket was soaked in blood near the inch-wide hole drilled through his right shoulder. His eyes rolled back in his head and circled around a bit. Quite a fascinating dance, but he was still conscious. Perhaps even coherent.

"Where next, my friend?"

Moon pointed to Armin's knees.

"Through the bone."

"Oh, joy. That should be quite loud. I might not hear his answers over the clatter. How about it, Armin?"

The idiot licked his lips and lapped up drops of splattered blood. He shadowed his eyes, but I knew how to reinvigorate our dialogue.

"Based on your previous answers, I know why you boarded that ship. You came here seeking revenge for your father's death. As I've told other men, revenge is a futile endeavor. It's like a meal of empty calories. Any satisfaction fades almost at once. So, let's go again. How did you learn about us?"

"No. No."

I stopped Moon from penetrating the first knee cap.

"Very well, Armin. Yes. We killed your father and his sidekick Vincente. My partner infected them at my request. That particular virus kills slowly and reduces a man to a quivering waste."

Armin's stare recaptured his original loathing. I finished my confession dripped in arrogance.

"In retrospect, Mando needn't have died. He never aggrieved us, but he was an obstacle to our ambition. Obstacles like him can't be allowed to interfere. You understand. Yes?"

"F-fucking malgado."

"Eh. That invective is thrown around much too liberally. It lacks the sting after a while. So, how did you learn about us?"

I gave Armin credit: Not only did he answer, but he leaned

forward as if prepared to spit in my face. Perfect.

"My father's friends told me what you did."

He was Horax. Not hard to deduce, but confirmation helped.

"Which was?"

"You lured us into a trap and killed dozens of us. You executed Senora Evelyn."

"Accurate so far. What else?"

"You started war between Horax and Poros. Many of my friends died because of you."

I stayed out of range of his saliva.

"We stirred the pot, but don't blame us for your little gang's horrible choices. Still. The line of causality does revert to Desperido. So, you learned our identities through your boss, Mateo Cardinale. Yes?"

His silence confirmed my suspicion.

"Did Senor Mateo die with your crew?"

Armin smirked.

"You will wish he did."

"Ah. So he was too much a coward to lead the assault. Not a problem. We know where he lives. What was the plan, Armin? After bombing the town, what next? Landing teams execute survivors?"

Again with the silent act.

"Hmm. With all the recent losses, you must've been promoted often. Too bad you didn't remain home. The Horax now have many more openings. Unless this wasn't solely a Horax operation. We know your ship entered worm at Conquillos Base. A very unlikely origin. Last we heard, it was under tight UNF security following the sniper incident a few weeks ago. Who else participated in this mission?"

I doubted we'd learn more from this asshole. He was an expendable gun who likely didn't know the scope of any alliance. If Cardinale wasn't onboard, others with the most to lose wouldn't have jeopardized their lives either. Our next move crystallized.

"Last chance, Armin. Names. Now."

"No. Never."

I shrugged and rose to my feet.

"I only knew your father for a few hours before I had him killed. Mando carried himself with a bit of flair. Ultimately, however, he was an animal, no better than your ordinary beast of burden. He lived under the long whip of the late Senora Evelyn. He died in her service, as you will die indentured to Senor Mateo. Very sad, Armin Salazar."

I left instructions inside Moon.

"Continue asking for names but expect no answers. Inflict pain until his misery reaches its pinnacle."

"Easy."

"Make sure he experiences indescribable agony up to his final breath, my friend. Then meet me in Control. We have work to do."

"How long should I play?"

I studied the unfortunate survivor. That was the universe, for you: Always trying to balance both extremes of the spectrum.

"Call it after ten minutes. I should have the command structure assembled by then."

"On it."

I waved to the unluckiest man on Azteca.

"Farewell, Armin. You'll die as forgotten as your father."

He cursed as he spit, but Moon's tools changed the equation. Armin's screams cut through the night, heard only by the lizards in the eastern desert. He would not be the last to die before sunrise.

I ordered Bett to summon her eight best fighters plus Ship and Genoa to Desperido Control. After everyone assembled, I threw open my pom and spread out a holoschematic of Hosta Grande Cardinale on the outskirts of Machado. I opened the proceeding with the biggest headline.

"This is our target, my friends. We will strike within the hour."

Bett was as shocked as anyone.

"The fuck, Raul? What is this place?"

"Shortly after the incident on Road Train 1492, Ilan and I planned a follow-up mission to silence all Horax leadership. We scanned the ranch with sighter drones and developed an assault strategy. We ultimately aborted the scheme in favor of a more nuanced approach in the city. It bought us time, which has now expired.

"Mateo Cardinale played a role in tonight's attack, but I believe he allied with more powerful entities, perhaps aligned with the UNF, the shipping guilds, or even the man we installed as Governor of Monteria Province. The crew met at Conquillos Base, which likely rules out separatists or Children of Orpheus.

"We need to know who they are. At this moment, anyone monitoring their mission has flown into panic mode. The ship did not have time to relay a distress signal. Comms and the transponder would have disappeared in a blink."

Bett nodded.

"Whoever's on the other end will assume the worst. You want to press the advantage while they're blind."

"Correct. I doubt Cardinale took lead. The Horax have suffered a sizable beating in recent weeks. He found a lifeline. We need to know not just the identity of his benefactors but the larger plan. Was the attack retribution, or something more profound? They intended to eliminate all life in this town."

Sgt. Manuel Kato, tapped to run security on Inuit Kingdom but recruited for this mission, sighed at the obvious conclusion.

"If not for the shields, they might have succeeded."

Genoa joined the conversation.

"We cut off the Horax at their knees months ago, Raul. They knew where to find us if they wanted payback. Why wait until now, after we've built an army?"

"Good question. Here's a better one: How did they not know about our defenses? The cloak is brilliant. Yes. It creates a mirage. But anyone who operates a worm-enabled transport of that class would not attack without having scouted the town. We own a barrage of sighter drones; they're no less capable."

Bett added: "Road trains pull in here every week, sometimes twice. All anyone had to do was ask the agents what they saw. From a tactical standpoint, nothing makes sense. They came out of worm too close, traveling too fast. Our sedans exit aperture at least five hundred meters outside the shield."

So many contradictions. How typically human.

"It's possible, Bett, they appointed a fool for a captain. But I believe the truth is more complex. We must do this now. Ilan?"

Moon designed the original scheme. His eyes twinkled when I gave him the floor. I felt confident he had quietly revised the original plan in his mind to reflect our current resources.

"Raul and I need two small strike teams. That's why you're here."

Bett shook her head.

"Ilan, that ranch is enormous. The security will be ..."

"Unimportant. You remember Todos Santos?"

"I do. But the topography gave you an advantage. What I see here is a flat terrain with neatly trimmed gardens and many open spaces. It will be infested with security."

She made a fair objection. Then again, Bett joined us long after we first dispensed with the Cardinale threat.

Moon pointed to locations north and south of the estate house.

"Raul and I will take out anyone with a heartbeat. The silence will allow us to invade undetected. The strike teams will enter the property here and here when we call for backup. Five of you will hold the perimeter. One will remain in contact with Bart's Nav if reinforcements arrive."

"And the others?" Genoa asked.

"Mateo Cardinale's extended family lives there," I said. "They'll be useful."

Everyone appeared to understand what I meant. Ship had not said a word, but he studied the ranch with a fixation.

"Anyone have a problem with our plan?" I asked.

Genoa raised her hand.

"Raul, from the time I joined the militia, you preached the three P's. Preparation, patience, poise. I don't have a doubt we got the last one covered. I know everyone here. We'll do the job. You say go, we go. And yeah, you got a handle on the logistics."

"What's your *but*, Genoa?"

"But we were hit forty minutes ago. I doubt we've found all the bodies. We're consumed by shock and grief. Raul, this feels like revenge. You said a counterstrike must be clinical, free of emotion."

She had me there. Or so she thought.

"Further proof you were a fine choice to run G'hladi. In most cases, you'd be right, my friend. But I don't intend to inflict death upon the Cardinales simply to counter our losses. We face an inflection point. Black Star has a new enemy, and I doubt tonight's attack will be the last. Cardinale is our only lead.

"He has the answers, and we must get to him before he and his ilk go to ground. We'll grieve our dead another day. Have I addressed your concern?"

Genoa broke into a liberal smile.

"You have, boss. I wanted to be certain you were doing this for the right reason in the right way."

Didn't recall a human questioning my authority in that vein. Moon did so frequently, of course. Genoa the go-getter continued to impress.

We explained the precise tactics, split the fighters into two teams headed by Genoa and Sgt. Kato. If we lost those two in battle, we'd have to install new leaders off world. Another personnel headache.

Eh. Low risk.

The teams raced to their modules to collect weapons. Bett adjusted our Black Alert defenses, which included landing Bart for our needs. I could've chosen another vehicle, but I so loved taking my first sedan into the fray.

Later, as we prepared to board, Elian caught up with us.

"Boss, I just heard. I should pilot Bart. I know it inside and out."

"No, my friend. You're retired from that sort of work. The town is counting on you. I'm counting on you. Yes?"

He dropped his shoulders but posed no objection.

Ship passed us without a word. I caught the kid before he boarded.

"Quite the birthday gift. Yes?"

He grunted. "You don't have to worry about me, boss. I can handle it. I'm ready."

"Good. There's a distinct possibility I'll be asking a great deal of you tonight. I expect you to demonstrate the man you've become. Yes?"

I saw emptiness in those eyes. Not the hint of reservation or moral confusion. We'd both learn the truth soon enough.

5

HUMANS WERE INEFFICIENT. Other times, they were just plain stupid. Mateo Cardinale protected his family and his ranch in the most stupid, inefficient way: He stocked it with humans carrying rifles. His wealth could have bought him a state of the art security system – one that even Moon and I might have struggled to penetrate.

Yeah, no. These cartel types died as they lived for centuries: With a gun in their hand. What wasted machismo.

Moon took the north. I claimed the south. Our goggles detected heat signatures. The rest, as they say, was easy pickings.

We were ghosts, slithering through the estate at fifty times the fastest man. We focused Ixoca's terraform matrix on each minion's heart. In our experience, exploding an organ required less precision than attacking blood vessels or nerves.

Line of sight within thirty meters did the trick.

It happened so fast, no one sensed trouble before they died. Most tipped over as if pushed by an invisible hand. We showed them mercy; how many would've someday died violently in the service of this ridiculous family?

I took no special pleasure in slaughtering humans this way. We had a patently unfair advantage, as befitting gods. The act itself was mechanical, like flipping off switches. It carried none of the thrill born in combat. It was as simple as it was predictable.

However, it saved time.

Of all the advantages I gained through the merge with Ixoca, this one I would miss the most.

As I reached the pool, which glistened in the night much like Ixoca's terraform shaft beneath Todos Santos, I saw the last two guards patrol nearby. The pool was empty, but a woman lay stretched out on a chair. She wore a swimsuit and wrapped her hair in a towel. She must have been thirty. I matched her against the database of images we had assembled over the months. She was Sara, the middle daughter.

She would've been excellent leverage. Unfortunately, one scream would complicate matters. Plus, we'd find more than ample bargaining power inside. After I took out the last goons with guns, Sara lapsed into a permanent sleep.

The mansion featured twelve bedrooms, eight water rooms, two kitchens, three dining rooms, two recreation rooms, two studies, a pool, and a solarium. Unless, of course, they added on after our first drone survey. We also knew the house contained a secure cam network controlled from the estate's central power cluster.

The moment we cleansed the grounds of human threats, Moon contacted our teams on Bart. I entered the power cluster adjacent to the east wing, transferred its live data spool to my goggles, and studied until I found our prime target. Then I disabled the cams. Bart glided whisper-quiet out of the shadows, landed one team north and the other south. My people converged on their designated positions.

Communicating through goggles, I delineated the targets inside. The five who would join us knew what they were looking for, as they had studied the surveillance images en route. Anyone of the Cardinale line suited our needs. I gave orders to shoot resisters.

Moon and I needed to acquire the prime target before the inevitable clamor. If Mateo felt even an inkling of trouble, he and the flunkies nearby might gum up our operation.

We entered the house an hour before midnight. Most of the family and staff had retreated to bed, but the patriarch hunkered down in a second-floor study with three men. We raced through the house and upstairs in a blur. I thought of the many other contexts where we might duplicate this behavior. An army seemed redundant.

Outside the closed study doors, I whispered in Genoa's mind.

"Round them up. I'll follow your progress."

Her team entered the house and took a more furtive approach to the bedroom suites.

"Ready for the show, partner?" I asked Moon as we unholstered our pistols and flipped up our goggles.

"You promise a good one?"

"Premium. You can take lead."

We each grabbed a lever and pulled. The dark-paneled study was brightly lit, allowing us to quickly identify the four men. Prime sat behind a grandiose desk which seemed appropriate for a man of great power and considerable testosterone. A second sat on the nearest sofa smoking a digipipe. Three and four reached inside their jackets. Oops. They gave themselves away.

Moon got to their hearts first. They collapsed like sculptures built on a fragile base.

We turned our weapons on the survivors.

"Those two weren't much help," I said with a chuckle. "Hire better bodyguards. I cannot overstate the value of quality staff. Right, partner?"

Moon laughed.

"Be the best, hire the best."

"Nice slogan, my friend. Learn it from me?"

"Yep."

"And right now, our best are inside this house. So, your options are limited, Senor Cardinale."

He lacked the grandfatherly aura of the last time we met. Mateo wanted to play hero but had enough common sense to know better.

"Who are you? How did you get into my ...?"

I waved him into silence.

"Yes, yes. The usual first questions. To be fair, I do believe this is the first time I've entered a man's home and threatened to kill his entire family." I massaged my beard. "It's been so long. I might have forgotten one of those fun adventures when I was a kid."

"*My family*. Wuh ... what have you done to them?"

He was predictably horrified but also seemed like one of those paranoid cunts who kept a pistol taped beneath his desk. We needed him breathing for a while longer.

"First, Senor, I'd like you to step out from behind the desk and join this well-manicured individual on the couch." When he hesitated, I added: "Your wife and children love you dearly."

That did the trick, thank you.

After Mateo took a seat and stared with the predictable combo of disdain and terror, Moon motioned toward a box on the old man's desk.

"Is that a humidor?" He asked the patriarch, who nodded.

I chuckled. "My partner is a lifelong connoisseur of cigars."

Moon opened the box and studied the brown tobacco sticks.

"Care for one, partner?"

"I'm good, thanks. Enjoy, my friend."

I reclined in a delightful chair with a silk cushion and a tall back meant for royalty. Fitting.

"Time for introductions, Senor. My name is Raul Torreta, and my equally vainglorious partner is Ilan Natchez. We are the administrators of a little organization known as Black Star."

Cardinale appeared to sink into the sofa cushion. More or less.

"No. You can't be. You're ..."

"Dead? Why are humans always in denial about the obvious? Before we move to the critical business of the evening, I have a question." I shifted my pistol toward the second fella. "Who are you, my friend? And please, do be specific."

He was daintily dressed, his tie and jacket well met even for so late in the evening. It contrasted with Cardinale, who wore no tie and had flung his jacket over the desk chair.

"Pino. Alfred Pino."

"And you are?"

"I am the family's chief solicitor."

"Ah. You bear a vague resemblance to the man himself. How are you related?"

Pino deferred to Cardinale, who nodded for him to continue.

"Second cousin."

"OK then. So, you must be the replacement for Jesus Limon, poor fellow. I met him at Conquillos a few months back. He didn't last as long as I predicted. I suspect you're of no more use than him."

I shot Pino twice in the chest. He slumped forward, smoke rising from his tidy little suit jacket.

"Let's face it," I told Cardinale. "Nobody loves solicitors. They're necessary in certain contexts, but would you give your life for one? No. I didn't think so."

"*Please*. Senor. Raul. You're making a mistake."

A cloud of deep blue smoke hovered around Moon.

"First impression, my friend?"

He nodded. "Smooth. A slow burner. I'll take the box."

"Excellent. You must have a sophisticated taste for the leaf, Mateo. We *are* on a first-name basis now. Yes?"

Mateo clasped his hands against his chest. I saw nothing about

44

religion in his biography, so prayer wasn't the old man's game.

"I'll do anything. Please. My family is not part of this."

"Directly?" I clicked my tongue against the roof of my mouth. "Not per se. But anyone born to the Cardinale name is expected to follow the family tradition. Yes?"

Mateo found a draught of courage. He leaned forward and rested his clinched fists on his thighs.

"I am the only one who can give you whatever you seek. Hurt them, and you gain nothing."

I laid the pistol in my lap. The cigar smelled quite lovely. A nutty bouquet. I'd have to try one on the return trip.

"Always humors me when men try to brave their way out of a hopeless predicament. Better than abject surrender, I suppose. Tell me, Mateo. How is your grandson Rafa?"

He stiffened like dry cement, and his skin turned as gray.

"How do ...?"

"The boy went through a difficult time a few months ago. Yes? Five of his mates were slaughtered in a pool while he watched. No one was ever charged for the crime. How's the kid holding up?"

I saw the gears turn until he reached an epiphany.

"*You* ... you were part of it."

"Actually." I pointed to Moon, who sat against the desk and enjoyed his smoke. "He's the best."

"It was quick," Moon said. "Those kids only felt a second of pain. Then they were gone. Your grandson almost cut into my line of sight. Close call. Answer my partner. How's he holding up?"

Mateo looked down to deliver a feeble response.

"He's ... he's a strong young man."

I looked around for something to drink. If Mateo had whiskey on par with his cigars ...

"Hmm. No doubt. After all, he's a Cardinale. So too were the other grandchildren – the ones you were watching at the park that day. I'm pleased you cooperated. Otherwise, Mateo ..."

"It was you? You sent the man who threatened my family?"

"Eh. After a fashion."

I longed for this moment. I always got a kick out of the facial reactions when we shapeshifted. The template inside my syneth core activated. I envisioned the dull man with gelled black hair parted down the middle. Slender nose, double chin, wire-frame glasses, humorless. Never did name the smug little prick.

"Hello, there," I announced in my new form. Mateo retreated into the cushion again. "That day, I demanded full Horax capitulation in all matters related to the shipping guilds, the incident on Roadway 9, and territory both east and south of Machado. You complied at first. But now you've obviously broken those terms. I said if you violated them, we would wipe the Cardinale name from history. Yes?"

I didn't care much for the squirrelly bastard, so I reverted to Raul. I'd grown quite fond of my gunslinger persona. Soon, I'd have to decide whether it would succeed off world.

Eh. A problem for another day.

"Do you remember what you asked when we shook on the deal?"

I'm sure he did, but Mateo had lost his tongue. It happens.

"You asked, 'Who are you?' I replied, 'Pray you never know.' Now you do." I crossed my legs and sighed. "Humans are poor listeners. Especially the ones who run empires. It's hard giving way when you stand atop the pyramid."

Mateo rediscovered his indignation.

"Leave him alone. Leave them all alone."

Predictable, but what else could he say? Bit late for an apology.

Throughout the conversation, I followed events elsewhere in the estate through Ship's and Genoa's eyes. Their team handled matters nicely, rounding up family members and a few nearby staff. Some resisted and took rifle butts upside the head, but a cacophony of pleas and screams never emerged. Had to love these Cardinales: They'd been taught how to handle themselves in a crisis.

I opened my pom and threw up holos from five bodycams. I expanded them so as to leave no confusion. Everyone from the matriarch to a pair of ten-year-old twin girls huddled in a recreation room. Most wore pajamas.

"You see, Mateo, you hold their fate in your hands. Ensure we don't exterminate three generations of Cardinales tonight."

Now he reached that piss-in-the-pants moment. His brief flicker of defiance vanished.

"No more killing, Raul. Tell me your price."

"Good. Good. Tonight, you and certain allies attempted to destroy my lovely little desert town. Please, no denials of your involvement. My intellect, while dwarfing your own, is not above being insulted."

"Yes. Anything you need to know."

"I will require names. Organizations. Dates. Locations. A crew. Leave out anything or anyone, and I'll know."

He grabbed his chest. Great, another potential heart victim.

"Would you like a glass of water, my friend?"

"Y-yes. Please."

"On it," Moon said with a delicious grin.

"Now, back to my terms, Mateo. I doubt you'll reveal everything. Just enough to create the veneer of transparency and protect yourself against retribution from your betrayed allies."

"No. You're wrong. I'll hold back nothing."

"That's correct. But I don't believe a dead solicitor and fearful family members will provide sufficient motivation. Ship, do you hear me?"

The kid came back. "Yes, boss."

"See the young man next to the billiard table? Wearing the checkered shirt."

"Gotcha, boss."

"His name is Rafa Cardinale. Sound familiar?"

I thought Mateo might try to jump me and commit suicide. I motioned for Moon to put down the glass of water and grab hold of the patriarch. The old man had seen enough of his cartel's handiwork to know my plan.

"No. No, please, Raul."

"Ship, I want you to shoot Rafa in the head. Now."

The kid did not hesitate. Without a response, he marched toward the young man of similar age. Rafa backed up a half-step, staring at the rifle. He raised his hands in a defensive posture.

"Hey, wait. I ..."

A green laser bolt cut a deep, black hole between the grandson's eyes. He collapsed against the wall, leaving a trail of blood as he sank to the floor, staring into the abyss.

Cries and shouts erupted from the other hostages, their wails now echoing through the house. Mateo grabbed his gut and bent over.

"Thank you, Ship. Now, I want you to pick any two hostages. Don't tell me who. When next you hear from me, kill them."

"On it, boss."

He said it with a cold, professional demeanor. Well done. Certainly not a kid any longer.

I focused on Mateo.

"Your grandson's death is on you, Senor Cardinale. You people never learn. Oh, well. Time to conduct the necessary transaction. If I detect even a crack in your story, the next two die. Yes?"

He wiped away his tears and nodded.

I opened the pom's recording device and waited until the old man drank his water. Moon grabbed the ex-solicitor and tossed his corpse onto the floor, taking a seat beside the patriarch. He smoked happily throughout the confession.

Mateo spoke for ten minutes uninterrupted. We responded with a handful of follow-up questions and finished our interrogation.

The intel was as remarkable as it was predictable. I had no reason to doubt the man. But with each new cross-stitch in the larger pattern, my conviction intensified as to the true force behind tonight's attack. I set my mind to the next stratagem and then to the issues awaiting us in Desperido.

When Mateo ran out of answers, I made my position clear.

"They'll be set free, my friend. Unfortunately, you will not. But I'm sure you knew."

I witnessed many enemies face death: Some with defiance, others with resignation, but most in tears. Mateo reacted as all emperors do in the moment before their fall.

With stunned disbelief.

Men like him lived forever. Others died in their name. Such was their place in the world.

Yeah, no.

"I'll give you the honor of selecting the method. How would you like it, Senor Cardinale?"

Life flickered from his chilled, pale features. He muttered without moving his lips.

"Excuse me? Speak up, please."

"Not the face," he said. "Not my face."

"Ah." I nodded to Moon, who walked behind the couch. "I'm sure we can accommodate. Thank you, Mateo. Farewell."

Moon's deft hands passed around Mateo like a conjurer creating an illusion. A red waterfall erupted from the old man's neck. He gurgled but didn't reach for the fatal wound.

He gave in to death. Smart.

Moon retracted the blade, which morphed into a hand. I pushed myself from the chair, which provided a delightful sitting experience.

"What do you think, my friend?"

Moon grabbed the humidor.

"You were right. Premium show. Lots of work to do, Royal."

"True. And not much time to complete it. At least we know the force of the headwinds."

I lied for Ixoca's benefit. The entire visit I designed for him. Though I dared not say it aloud just yet, the conclusion was undeniable: Ixoca masterminded everything. I knew why he ordered the attack on the Fort of Inarra and tonight on Desperido. The real problem was in understanding how he pulled it off.

Theories. I loved them so. Better yet, I loved proving them.

I contacted my team leaders.

"Genoa, Kato: We're done here. Prepare for extraction. Kato, have you planted our gifts?"

"The garden is full, boss."

"Outstanding. Ship?"

"Yes, boss?"

"Kill the two you selected."

"On it."

He dropped a pair of middle-aged women. Staff, I assumed.

"Genoa," I said over renewed screams, "tell the hostages to wait five minutes after we leave. If anyone exits prematurely, they will meet the same fate."

"Gotcha, boss. See you at the rendezvous."

And then, the special visual effects.

These pricks had it coming.

6

NEVER CARED MUCH FOR FIREWORKS. When I was a kid on Hokkaido, my limited friends and family oohed and aahed at the sight. I wanted to like the dancing sparkles, but they felt superficial for reasons I couldn't define. Fireballs, on the other hand, captured my attention. They said something had gone terribly wrong. The world fell into chaos; people died. Even better: They weren't synchronized.

My love of fire paled next to Moon's, of course. He watched entire planets roast with the greatest zeal and long thereafter described the apocalyptic bouquet. He was insane back then. *Maximos deos* with a hunger for random, widescale devastation. He had since mellowed somewhat.

Still, we both found satisfaction watching from a distance as fiery flowers erupted around the base of Hosta Grande Cardinale. We didn't erase the family from existence, as we threatened, but we made good on the largest symbol of their faux empire.

Bart's last scan before we left the area showed hostages escaping the blaze. Nothing but the shirts on their backs. Fitting.

"One battle down," I told the crew. "More to come."

Ship spoke for everyone.

"That will teach them to fuck with Black Star."

"Point taken, Ship. Though I doubt those poor sods have any idea who hit them. At least we have answers, enough to prepare for the battles ahead."

"Cardinale gave you good intel?" Genoa said.

"Oh, yes. The entire conspiracy against Black Star. And a bit more than he intended." I chuckled. "Said it before and will again: Family is the best leverage. When faced with the deaths of loved ones, most humans do your bidding. Betray confidences, deliver classified data, remember what they had for breakfast ninety-eight days ago. Far more effective than torture."

"What's our next move, boss?"

No need to get ahead of ourselves.

"We'll discuss it in the morning, after we've dealt with the full scope of what happened in our town."

I pushed Elian's and Bett's eyes aside during the mission but saw and heard just enough to understand. There'd be no talk of victory or retribution when we landed.

As we neared Desperido, I invited Ixoca to share his views.

"You heard Cardinale, my friend. Did you detect any gaps or errors in his story?"

She pixelated blue above the Nav board. I hadn't seen the feminine form in more than a week.

"I only know a few of the actors, but the chain of events he described seems credible."

Except for the missing ingredient.

"Any thoughts as to why the ship exited worm too close?"

"Raul, do not overthink. It could have been nothing more than a miscalculation. A tight terrestrial jump is a fragile maneuver."

Huh. You *would* say that, Ixoca.

"Possibly. Until I know for sure, I intend to investigate. Any word yet from your generals?"

"Empty responses, I'm afraid. A few have said they will poke around. Cardinale's confession fully exonerates my Children."

So it appeared. Awfully damn convenient, too.

The last leg of our trip was quiet but for one excellent suggestion from Sgt. Kato. I took his proposal to Bett, who greeted us alone upon arrival. I spoke to her before anyone disembarked.

"I said this once before, but now I know for certain: The Horax will never concern us again, Stopper. We'll discuss details in the morning. In the meantime, these teams want to know how they can be of immediate assistance."

She nodded. "Blood. The synthetics are low. The medpod wasn't equipped for so many."

I turned to my crew.

"There you have it. Report to Mod 3."

"Yes, boss," they said in unison.

A victory celebration it most definitely was not. Just like those six years fighting Swarm.

We walked into town with Bett, surveying the mess. The fires were out, although the largest ship debris smoldered. Central avenue, earlier the site of a birthday party, now doubled as a makeshift morgue. Sheets covered the bodies.

"How many?" Moon asked.

"Twenty-nine. Another twenty are holding on by their goddamn fingernails. Thirty more with minor burns, flesh wounds, nothing to scream about."

I asked, "Is everyone accounted for?"

We stopped at the morgue's edge.

"Elian took charge of that. Told me ten minutes ago he finished the residency check of the western bunkers."

Good to hear he took my advice to heart.

"Most deaths occurred there, I assume?"

Bett pulled on a cheroot.

"Seventeen. The one bit of good news: The number would've been ten times higher if most weren't topside for the party. The engine array incinerated those bunkers."

"Amazing, isn't it? The enemy struck at the height of something that only occurs every two or three weeks."

"Luck was on our side."

I stared at the covered bodies.

"Was it?"

"Point taken, Raul."

She missed my point. Bett, like most humans, didn't understand: Luck was always a product of causality's knot. It required help.

"On top of everything else," I said, "we have a housing crisis."

"Already working it. Elian is meeting with the Sergeants of Mods 7 through 12. With most of our forces off world, we have space to accommodate two hundred. We'll double up where possible."

"Good. They won't be packed in for long. We'll expedite transfers."

I remembered Lumen's parting words: "In a few months, Desperido will be an empty shell. A hole in the desert." She wasn't far off.

"One more thing, Stopper. Suspend Black Alert. Gray will suffice."

She went full-on apoplectic.

"The fuck? Raul, if other ships exit worm, we have the firepower to bring them down *outside* the shield."

"There won't be another one, at least not for several days."

"How can you be certain?"

"Mateo Cardinale. The people behind this attack had one shot. They failed. As far as they know, we destroyed their vessel. When they send drones to investigate, they'll see the oasis dome intact – and no sign of wreckage. The mystery will hold them at bay."

She blew smoke out of a crimp in her lips.

"That's a hell of an assumption. You believed Cardinale?"

"I did. Agree, Ilan?"

My partner concurred. "He flipped on everyone to save his family."

"Fine. I don't like it, but it's your call."

"Thank you. What of our material losses?"

"Little of consequence. Four chasers, five rifters. All the critical assets are good to go."

"And what of their ship? Gleaned any evidence?"

"Definitely UNF design. Originally a supply transport. Saw many like it during the war. Significantly modified. By whom and how recent, not possible to say. Best guess? SI had a hand in this."

Maybe. I needed time to piece it together with Cardinale's tale and a few other scraps of evidence.

"I intend to review the secure cams tonight."

"What do you hope to find?"

"Uncertain, my friend."

Actually, I had very specific notions. One thing never sat right with me. The cams would confirm or deny my suspicion.

"Bett, I want you and Elian to inform the town: Everyone who is mobile will meet here at sunrise."

"On it. Should we tell them why?"

I tried to avoid a condescending glare.

"The answer should be self-evident. Attendance is compulsory."

"Will do. I hope you have some strong words, Raul. Morale has never been lower."

Moon interjected.

"They've been winning for too long. They're soft."

Bett knew better than to debate Moon. He was harsh, I suppose, but he wasn't wrong. The moment humans believe they can't lose, a crushing defeat becomes inevitable. The body count for Black Star and our enemies had only just begun to accrue.

Back in our bunker, I opened my pom and tapped into Desperido Control's data spools.

"This might take a while, my friend."

Moon laid back on the bed and selected a fresh smoke from Cardinale's humidor.

"You think it's an inside job, Royal."

"The thought occurred to me, but I wish it were so simple. We'd haul out the traitor at sunrise and burn him alive."

"I don't buy it, partner. We've had absolute control. We track every comm in and out. And our eyes ..."

"Are damned near everywhere. I agree. The one we're looking for likely has no idea."

Moon grunted. "Only one suspect comes to mind."

"In retrospect, it makes perfect sense, my friend. I'll be interested to know who pulled it off and how. Either way, this morning will offer many challenges."

For two hours, I reviewed the spools, secure cam feeds, and the invader before it disintegrated against the shield. Alongside Cardinale's story, the evidence filled in most gaps. The real trick would be orchestrating my next move without Ixoca knowing I was on to him.

I needed to lure him into a false sense of security, which proved difficult given my intellectual brilliance. Would the Jewel accept that I was unable to see the universe through the stars?

As sunrise neared, I closed my pom and discussed the upcoming ceremony. I proposed we take advantage of the moment and reinforce our power before Desperidans doubted us.

We stood at the entrance to our home and watched the crowd form.

"Would you like to say a few words, partner?"

Moon sighed. "That's your job, Royal. You brought them together once before. Same general location, as I recall."

The night he mentioned — when I spoke before the Circle and used the care workers' pain to unite the larger tribe — seemed ages ago. Humans bonded over unexpected troubles, but the covenant rarely endured. They weren't as fond of peace and unity as they claimed.

"When our words are finished," I told Moon, "we'll leave them with a once in a lifetime memory. C'mon."

We joined Elian and Bett on central avenue. The bodies of our dead were surrounded on three sides by a blend of contractors and fighters. The sun's first orange rays pierced through low-hanging clouds along the horizon.

"Is everyone present?" I asked bleary-eyed Elian. Like much of the town, he did not sleep last night.

"Should be, boss. I assigned house monitors to nudge stragglers."

"Very good. Commander?"

"All but four. One officer manning Control, the others flying Gray

Alert. They're watching on secure cam."

"Fine. Have you chosen your words carefully?"

Bett cleared her throat with a dry cough.

"Not much good at this, Raul. Never was."

We occupied the same boat, but her excuse felt limp.

"An officer doesn't write 'excellent at funeral oratory' on a job application. But it's an unavoidable feature of command."

"Don't I know it. I have the honors?"

"You do."

She stiffened her shoulders and tucked hands behind her back.

"I wouldn't stand a chance if you were the opening act."

After that insightful snark, Bett stepped forward and addressed the town.

"Last night, we celebrated on this street. Then cowards attacked us without warning or provocation. They killed thirty-one of us."

Two more died overnight.

"Ten fought under my command," Bett continued. "But everyone we lost was a valued member of our community. We have served each other's needs in ways ... well, in ways I never thought possible.

"We formed something unique in Desperido despite our wildly different backgrounds. That sort of bond finds a place deep in your heart and never leaves.

"Those of us who fought the Swarm know what I mean. We had no interest in each other until we needed each other. We trusted our lives to our brothers and sisters even when we weren't sure the next guy knew what in ten hells he was doing. We fought on the lines, we fought inside two-man Hornets, we fought on warships firing at each other from point-blank range.

"When the war ended and we returned home, not one of us forgot. Even if we never saw each other again, we'd always share that indefinable bond."

Bett impressed me with her composure in the moment. She untucked her hands and held them out to the dead.

"These people will always be with us, even if we didn't know every name or every story. History will forget Desperido, but we will not. History won't mark what happened last night, but we will."

She pumped her chest.

"We can't remove the bond if we tried. As for the cowards who did this ... they attacked because they're afraid of us. These are the same people who want to tear this world apart. The same ones who dishonored our service to Azteca. The same ones who forced many of you contractors to flee into the desert.

"We'll have justice. For the dead *and* the living. It's already begun."

Hmm. On the whole, her speech delivered the goods. However, Bett made a considerable leap with her final claim. Perhaps she felt the propaganda would motivate the town. She might've been right. But *justice*? A mere euphemism for revenge.

When Bett rejoined us, I whispered:

"Strong opening. My work is cut out for me."

These people heard me wax poetic on more than one occasion, while Bett's stern but thoughtful words came as a surprise. She carried much of the heavy lifting, so I trimmed my planned remarks.

I opened with a lie.

"Ilan and I have always loved the desert. It's unchanging and unceasing in an otherwise chaotic universe. It's clean." I chuckled. "Even though we brush red dust from our boots every day and grumble about it, we remain. The desert is quiet. When the lizards sing at night, they don't disturb our sleep. Rather, we hear a melody they have sung unaltered for centuries, and it delivers a measure of peace.

"The desert brings clarity and demands purpose. We who found our way to Desperido – by choice or circumstance – discovered a secret hidden to humans who do not understand the desert's power. Far from the clamor of proper society, we are forced to look inward. Forced by the quiet to hear the echoes of truth. To confront our purpose.

"Those who thrive on clamor fear those who have found clarity of purpose. As Commander Ortiz said, they're afraid of us. They came to eliminate us. To raze Desperido to the ground. They failed. They will always fail. Even after this town disappears from the map – and that fate seems inevitable – they will continue to fail. And we will continue to terrify them."

I held Desperido in my hands. But what were words without dramatic interpretation? So, I lifted my hands toward the morning sky, where the few remaining stars hovered near the western horizon. Then I preached.

"Up there! Over there! This direction and that! North on Roadway 9 to Machado and beyond. From the capitals of Azteca to the jungles of Indonesia Prime to the glaciers of Inuit Kingdom to the megacities of Earth and Catalan. We'll demonstrate clarity of purpose.

"They'll speak of Desperido and Black Star with both terror in their hearts alongside a healthy measure of respect. They will remember us for generations, even if this town has turned to ash. The desert will remember because the desert will contain *our* ash."

I pointed to the dead.

"These men and women found refuge in Desperido when all others turned their backs. The path ended here, and here is where they will live forever among the unchanging and unceasing desert."

Moon joined me to create a memory. I thought about giving Bett a heads-up as to whether we might violate any of her soldiers' last wishes. I decided against it. A soldier who died at sea used to be buried there; one who died in space was sent off to the stars. These humans chose to spend eternity blended with the dust.

"Farewell, my friends. Forever in our hearts."

Moon and I morphed our right hands into pure syneth, which converted to fire flickers containing a special accelerant. In the past, we customized cigars for these moments. Such a tool was better suited to individual disposal. This morning, we required two things: Speed and a massive wave of heat.

A vision and a memory.

I stood over what remained of Saul's body. Moon took position two rows away. We acted in unison.

The flicker shot a blast of accelerant that penetrated Saul and raced through his torso like wildfire. Then we ran at top speed, fire incinerating the corpses as if set ablaze all at once.

Desperidans up front tried to shield their faces from the intense heat. Many fell back into the crowd, but none ran and all recovered. Like others we incinerated, these flames consumed the flesh quickly then faded, leaving behind thirty-one small piles of ash.

All the burning corpses I witnessed during war emitted a putrid stench. Yet this fire cleansed the body so quickly as to leave a clean, sterile odor. And even that dissipated on the lightest breeze.

I watched beside Moon, Elian, and Bett as the last embers drifted into the morning sky. If our dramatics failed to hold Black Star together, I'd take the blame. Yet I'd wager our burgeoning empire just took an important step forward.

It was a lovely resolution to a dark night in our young history.

I'd have felt better about it if I didn't know the Commander of Black Star forces was a spy.

7

THE TABLE OF TRUST PLUS ONE met inside Desperido Control two hours later. Saul's absence touched a nerve. Damn, I'd miss his eloquence. I'd never known anyone who attempted to converse with me at the same linguistic level.

Moon and I took the head chairs, as usual. Bett and Genoa sandwiched around Sgt. Manuel Kato, who I invited to this meeting as a necessary one-off. Ship and Elian occupied the other side.

"My partner and I made some important decisions." I focused on our somewhat recovered drug lord. "Elian, you will take over Saul's duties at once."

He shouldn't have been surprised, yet his response lacked the usual Elian overconfidence.

"Yes, boss. I ... I can't replace Saul, but I'll give it a rip."

"Priorities have changed, Elian. After everyone finds suitable housing, begin the interview process for transfers. Start with your team. There's no point in trying to reconstitute the lost facilities here. The future of Motif production is off world."

Poor fella was run ragged. No more disaster-fueled adrenaline to hold him in top form.

"OK. I ... who do I coordinate with for the transfers?"

"Link your team into the digiform and send them out among the civilians only. We'll need a full accounting of their preferences within two days. They can join Black Star, settle off world, or find a cozy hiding spot on Azteca. When the list is compiled, you'll work with Ilan to develop a transport schedule."

Elian coughed through his response.

"What kind of ... *timetable* ... what kind of timetable are we looking at, boss?"

"Eight days. I want the civilian population gone in eight days."

Everyone except Moon gasped.

"So soon?" Genoa said. "I thought we had months, not days."

"Oh, we have years. Decades. But not here. Desperido was never more than a waystation, my friend. I realize you called this place home for many years, but it must die to ensure our continued success."

Ship seconded my sentiment.

"Can't leave this planet soon enough."

Moon followed suit.

"Our work here is compromised. Too many eyes on our business."

"And, as Ilan and I discovered last night, those eyes are not limited to Aztecan cartels and insurgent wannabes. Elian, will you commit to the timetable?" He wobbled a bit but not from a hangover. "You're clearly exhausted. Do you need to report to Mod 3?"

"No, boss. I'll get it together. It's just ... I ain't eaten in a spell. The phasic meds ... they ..."

I cut him off. "Understood. Get something to eat. Rest. Then assemble your team. Eight days, my friend."

He rose from his chair like a tattered creature twice his age.

"You got my word, boss. I'll see it done."

"Good. You're dismissed."

If I were human, I likely wouldn't have pushed Elian so hard. But he needed a fair dose of humbling before that narcissistic streak lured him into life-threatening trouble again.

After he left, Bett posed the logical military question.

"What do I tell the fighters? How long before they clear out?"

"That, my friend, is a touch more complicated. Certain tasks remain, and we have the forces at hand for those jobs. Moon and I will sit down with you later to discuss the rotation plan."

Among other things ...

"Raul, last night you told me there was no imminent threat. The people behind the attack failed at their one chance. What haven't you said?"

Oh, so very much, Stopper.

"Patience, Bett. I'll come to it."

She wasn't satisfied. Bett rarely was, but for reasons I only now began to understand.

"As long as you have a sensible plan, Raul, I can work with it."

"Trust me, we have no interest in risking the welfare of our army. We don't move forward without them. Which brings me to the intel we gathered at Hosta Grande Cardinale. Before I divulge these secrets, I remind you that everything discussed here is classified."

I focused on Kato, who admitted to surprise at his inclusion. Only Bett's closest lieutenants – Tracer Tolan and Inky Sisal – joined the table before today. They currently oversaw operations on Bolivar and Indy Prime.

"Sergeant, you're here because of the fine job your team did last night. We also believe your expertise in explosives will better serve us in the final operations on Azteca. So, for now, we're rescinding your assignment to Inuit. Any questions?"

Kato was a mild-mannered fella of forty, one of those officers who whipped people into shape with his eyes rather than his mouth.

"I'm at your service, boss." To Moon, he added: "Boss."

Moon appreciated those little touches; most Desperidans forgot we shared command of Black Star. Then again, humans gravitated toward the fellas who ran their mouths most often.

"Here's the story, my friends. We have no reason to believe any of it is false. In fact, the limited research we've conducted supports Cardinale's narrative.

"Five weeks ago, our snipers killed ten protestors at Conquillos Base. As expected, blame fell upon the UNF. Right-wing separatists claimed the outsiders were encroaching upon Aztecan sovereignty.

Their voices are now louder than ever.

"The cartels intensified their territorial wars and the battle over who would own the strongest arsenal for the so-called coming insurgency. Black Star set these actions into motion in order to remain unnoticed amid the clamor. Our strategy was working.

"However, one week after the Conquillos incident, a man who had accompanied the UNF delegation secretly met with Mateo Cardinale, Esteban Poros, and Julio Innez."

Genoa interrupted.

"They head the cartels at war with each other. Why would they meet with anyone in the UNF?"

"Because he wasn't UNF. The man's name is Shad Abdelmani from Euphrates. Consultant to UNF Ground Operations; former rep to the Interstellar Congress; before that, military contractor. In his younger days, a radical figure. Cardinale said Abdelmani talked openly about his time fighting for an independent Euphrates. He admired what certain groups on Azteca and other worlds were doing. He claimed to have no love for the People's Collectorate."

Bett said, "He's a hypocrite. What's he playing at?"

"You know the answer, just as well as Cardinale."

Bett's eyes expanded.

"He's SI."

"Almost certainly, though it's not likely we'll ever prove it without a confession. SI keeps a healthy distance from their covert operatives. Abdelmani told the cartel heads they were being manipulated by a third party. He claimed to know who was behind their troubles and vowed to eliminate the problem. He said the cartels would receive justice for having been wronged."

Genoa beat Ship to the punch:

"He was talking about us. Black Star."

"He provided proof we operated out of Desperido, that we killed Anton Cherry, Judge Barron, and Maris Sylva. He said the same man who manipulated the Poros and Horax cartels into war also killed Evelyn Cardinale and several ranking Horax lieutenants. After that,

Evelyn's brother Mateo became a highly motivated client."

Sgt. Kato asked: "What was Abdelmani's price?"

"After he ended Black Star, the cartels in question were to stand down. Of course, they'd receive a huge financial windfall. In the future, they would publicly support pro-Collectorate candidates to high office. All this, while working behind the scenes to support the separatist movements."

"Wait," Ship said. "This asshole was playing for both sides?"

"He pitched a credible future to these men. He said a galactic conflict was inevitable. Their power would grow exponentially if they came out of that conflict on the winning side."

Genoa asked, "I'm confused. Is he working on behalf of SI? Why would the government support insurgents?"

"It wouldn't," Moon said, his first words since we convened. "This cunt is playing a long game for his own benefit."

"We believe he operates on several worlds as a double agent," I added. "He uses SI resources while fattening his bank account. It's quite a lucrative and frankly ingenious scheme."

Except it was not Abdelmani's idea. That little revelation I pushed aside for now. Better to save it when we were alone with our traitor.

"Bottom line, my friends: The cartels bought in to the plan. Abdelmani told them Desperido was protected by a security shield, but he would provide a ship with the firepower to bring it down. He requested each cartel deliver a small team of motivated assassins to act as exterminators.

"He used his SI resources to order an unregistered, modified transport to Conquillos, where the teams rendezvoused. Cardinale said he sent five Horax agents, including the vengeful son of Mando Salazar, a nuisance we killed months ago. Poor Mateo made a ghastly error because that son survived the crash, providing a critical link. Causality ties a wicked knot, my friends."

The table took a moment to absorb the details before Bett said:

"Who flew the ship? Was Abdelmani onboard?"

"Doubtful. Cardinale queried Abdelmani about the ship and its crew. Abdelmani said his people were experienced operatives. He told Cardinale, 'My man Raeger will do the job. Desperido stands no chance.' This is important because Ilan and I know of Col. Raeger. He's SI, and he took part in the mission that destroyed the Fort of Inarra."

That tidbit threw the room into a tizzy. Moon and I never told anyone what we saw that night six months ago on our private security feed or what Ixoca revealed to us about the attack. Now seemed like a good time to open that door.

"We believe Abdelmani has known about Ilan and me for quite some time. Moreover, we believe he ordered the bombing."

After you got to him, Ixoca!

I expected the Jewel to appear at any second. He had to realize we were about to expose his treachery.

Ship asked, "How does he know your true nature?"

The kid likely assumed Abdelmani learned about us through our employment with the President. Smartly, he left out that bit. After all, I promised to shoot him in the head if he told anyone.

"Ilan and I are well traveled. We impacted lives long before we came to Azteca. A man with Abdelmani's skills and resources must not be underestimated. Months ago, we learned of a somewhat legendary figure among insurgents across the Collectorate. Codename: Q6. One person. Well placed. Working to bring down the galactic government from the inside. Or so went the urban legend.

"The concept motivated both the ambitious and the seditious. We believe Abdelmani is Q6."

At worst, I told them a fib to hide the greater lie. Ixoca's original Jewel name was Q6, but he couldn't have created the legend on his own. He needed a human who fit the necessary tag; someone outside the Children of Orpheus who would build a living mythology across a multiplanetary network. How and when Ixoca got to Abdelmani posed a pair of fun questions which we intended to ask our favorite Jewel.

Bett rapped her knuckles on the table.

"That's a hell of a story Cardinale told. Let say it's true down the line. One big problem, Raul. A crew like he assembled would not fuck up worm coordinates. They would not exit aperture so close to a shield they knew existed."

Did the answer hit Bett upside the head during or after she said the words aloud? She cursed under her breath and shifted her eyes around the table. Genoa, Ship, and Sgt. Kato caught up quickly.

"Goddamn," Genoa said. "They'd only exit that close if they believed the shield was down."

Kato continued: "We have a mole."

"Traitor," Bett said in a moment of considerable irony.

I decided to lighten the funereal atmosphere.

"Bad news? Yes. We have a traitor in our midst. Good news? The traitor failed. Consequently, we live to fight another day."

"Who is it?" Ship said. "Got to be someone with access to the shield controls."

"One would think, my friend. But that narrows our list to fifteen. Actually, fourteen." I hated saying it. "Saul had access."

"What's the plan?" Bett said with a perfectly straight face.

"In a moment, I'll ask most of you to leave. Ilan and I will remain here with Stopper to develop a strategy. We intend to do this quietly. You can well imagine what happens if word seeps out. Paranoid humans do not present well."

Moon added, "Far as they know, we got everything under control. Go about your business and lift morale. Ship, check in on Elian. He needs to pop his ass in gear."

"On it, boss."

"What about me?" Genoa said. "I'm supposed to leave for G'hladi in three hours."

"Change of plan," I told her. "You'll be leaving, but for Inuit in place of Sgt. Kato. You wanted a more challenging command, and G'hladi can wait. It's quiet. Your number two can handle it."

"Honestly, I'd rather be here, boss. I have a bad feeling there's trouble coming our way."

"You're not wrong, Genoa, but we have everyone we need."

She wanted to protest further, but the long sigh said she thought better of it.

"Just remember, I'll only be an hour's jump away."

Moon spoke for me: "If we need commanders, we'll call you first."

I turned to the kid.

"Ship, final thoughts?"

He slitted his eyes and tightened those jowls.

"When you find the malgado, let me take him out."

"Noted, my friend. The three of you are dismissed."

They left us alone to conclude a most challenging – and dare I say it, unsatisfying – chain of events. A twist of fate allowed us to uncover answers far more quickly than we had any right to. In one respect, I would've preferred not knowing. But there were no genies, no bottles, and no takebacks.

Only the nasty truth.

Bett spoke first.

"They might've missed it, but I know you two are holding back."

"Oh, my friend. Ilan and I hold many truths in reserve. Some because humans can't handle them, and others because they'll have strategic value someday."

Stopper threw up her hands.

"Fine. Which one is it this time?"

"A mix of both, but primarily the latter."

The moment arrived, but Ixoca had yet to appear. What in ten hells was he waiting for? He had to know our next move. Not even interested in defending himself?

Yeah, no.

"Whichever, Raul. Spill it. Then we need to track down the mole and get this shit sorted."

I unholstered a pistol and laid it on the table. Moon did the same.

"Don't have to," Moon said. "We already know who it is."

Bett was not an attractive woman on a good day. Rage turned her into something downright monstrous.

8

AFTER THE ACCUSATION SANK IN, Bett unloaded on us. Moon and I allowed her a moment for the expected indignation and resentment. She pushed back her chair and ignored our weapons. We listened without objection.

"Bad enough you nearly got me killed on 1492. Ruined my career and my life. Now, after what? Five months I been here? I recruit your army ... because you damn well weren't building Black Star without me ... convince my people it's worth following a pair of gods into every kind of criminal mischief ... go in all the way so I can set things straight with the assholes trying to rip this planet apart ..."

She waved a finger back and forth like a pendulum.

"After all I gave, you two think I've been *what*? Working for the other side? Think I'd open the front door so the enemy could slaughter every goddamn body in this town?"

What was left but to laugh in our faces? In her shoes, I would've done the same. In some cultures, the guilty proclaimed their innocence by saying they were victims of a 'witch hunt.' Only solid proof of their crimes forced them to retreat. Usually.

"Stopper," I said with a dulcet, forgiving tone. "Please sit."

"Why, Raul? So you can tell me how you intend to pin this shit on me? How you'll make me disappear and cover up the real reason I ain't around anymore? Lose me, lose your army."

Moon reached for a cigar while I grabbed my pom.

"She's all yours," he whispered inside my mind.

"There's no reason why we can't double-team, my friend."

"Bett's right. You screwed the pooch on 1492. She isn't here without you, Royal."

I smirked. "I hate when you remind me of my errors, few though they may be."

Bett continued: "The fuck if I let you brand me a traitor. I cashed in my life for Black Star."

I crossed my so-called arms and hit her with a parental are-you-done-yet stare.

"Bett. Stopper. We haven't leveled a charge. But I must show you something. Please, do sit."

She complied with eyes full of fury.

I opened my pom and raised the holo containing my evidence.

"Last night, something bothered me about the way I was informed of the approaching danger. You said, 'We have a problem. Incoming wormhole.' To which I asked, 'Unauthorized?' You replied, 'Yes. Five seconds to aperture.' I'm sure you recall the moment."

"Yeah. So? That's what happened."

"At that point, Bett, we were helpless. Fate intervened, and the ship exited worm too close to the shield. But here's the problem. I reviewed the data spools. Their terrestrial jump lasted nineteen seconds. Our tracker detected it one second after they entered worm. It projected the course and sounded an alarm two seconds later. You notified me nine seconds afterward."

She threw out her arms.

"What's your point, Raul?"

"You had proof that an unauthorized, potentially hostile vessel was en route, but you did not warn anyone until it was too late. Protocol required you to activate the missiles for immediate intercept."

"This is why you think I'm a traitor? Because I hesitated? Raul, did it ever occur to you that maybe I was trying to verify the data? That I was probably shocked at what I saw coming."

As an opening salvo, yes, my case was weak. Time to prove it.

"*Probably* is an interesting word. Don't you remember?"

"All hell came crashing down. No. I don't remember my exact thoughts in those first seconds."

"I suppose you don't. Tell me, Bett. When did you relieve the duty officers for them to join the party?"

She grimaced at my change in direction.

"Wuh? I ... half an hour before."

"Did you make the decision on the spur of the moment?"

Bett opened her mouth to respond but caught herself. For an instant, I detected confusion.

"I ... I don't know. I thought they earned it. They missed the last two parties. I didn't want the duty rotation to screw them out of a good time again."

"A compassionate leader. Lovely. You entered the Control Center and did what for the next twenty-eight minutes?"

"Well ... what the hell you think? I ... I watched the trackers and monitored comms."

"You don't sound convinced. Here. Take a look."

I expanded the secure cam holo, starting from the moment she entered. Bett pulled up a chair and adjusted the sharpness on the monitors. She placed both hands on the counter in front of the comms transceiver and danced her fingers to a beat. This continued unabated for two minutes until I asked:

"Did you ever play piano?"

"The fu ...? Yes. I ... I do that whenever I'm alone. It helps me concentrate. I ..."

"OK. So, you remember this?" She nodded without confidence. "Watch, Bett."

I slowly sped up the replay. She didn't alter her position for twenty-five minutes. Her fingers rapped to the same rhythm.

"You ignored the wormhole tracker until right here, at one hundred seconds before the attack."

Bett had swiveled to her left and leaned forward, scanning the holobank that watched for any wormhole activity in the Aztecan system. She no longer played the piano.

"Watch this, my friend."

At sixty-five seconds before the attack, Bett extended her left hand to the adjacent holo.

"The shield controls. See where your hand is located?"

"I don't remember doing that."

I zoomed closer.

"Your index finger is an inch away from bringing down the shields. It points like an arrow. It needs only a signal from your brain."

The counter dropped.

Thirty seconds. Twenty-five. Twenty. Fifteen. Ten.

Suddenly, Bett snapped to. She cursed, dropped that index finger, and notified me of the impending danger.

I ended the playback and awaited her response. Only one reaction would convince me I was right about her. She delivered.

Bett fell back into her chair, eyes glazed over. This time, water glistened in her one natural eye.

"That never happened, Raul. I ... that isn't right. It's a trick, Ilan. I'm telling you both, I don't remember anything but the last seconds."

Yeah, about right.

"The cam doesn't lie, my friend. The proper question is, what truth is it telling us? Ordinarily, I'd say it proves you had a change of heart. But these aren't ordinary times, and we aren't ordinary people. The other option, perhaps better suited to your predicament: You had no control over your actions. Both, however, carry considerable baggage. You see our problem?"

She buried her face in her hands. I didn't envy the woman. She was either a two-faced cunt caught in the act, or she was an involuntary tool for the enemy. Nothing good to come of either.

Yeah, no. The truth sported a more complicated mask. Now felt like an excellent opportunity for Ixoca to explain himself. I wanted him to arrive on his own terms rather than at my behest. He had to know I would unmask him.

Still nothing.

"The moment is difficult, Stopper, but set aside your frustration. Examine the issue from our point of view. Abdelmani could not have acquired such detailed information on Black Star without inside help. The crew of that ship expected our shields to be lowered. You cleared out Control shortly beforehand and literally were a fingertip away from destroying the town.

"You walked into Desperido five months ago bearing a grudge against me but willing to put it aside if I provided a better life than the one you left behind. That occurred seventeen days after Saul and I met Horatio Vargas. During that meeting, he referenced your plight with Montez Shipping. At the time, I thought it strange.

"Two days after we allowed you to stay here, a road train arrived with a corrupt auditor you just happened to know. You unraveled his duplicity and gained favor. You made yourself at home inside the cantina, serving drinks and learning all you could about our contractors. Then you agreed to help us build the army, ensuring your position.

"When Ilan and I consider these events in their totality, the skeptic says they form a pattern. An enemy willing to play the long game plants an agent in our midst. She gains our trust and allows us to flourish until the enemy decides to take us down. She's willing to finish her mission until the final seconds, when at last she has reservations. She simply cannot go through with it. Bett, do you see how we might reach such a conclusion?"

Bett wasn't an innocent woman facing a firing squad, but I suspect she felt as helpless. She sat up straight and composed herself. She glanced at Ilan, then me, then the holo.

"Yeah. I see. In some insane, paranoid reality, it makes sense. Except none of it happened, Raul. I've been straight with you from day one. I murdered people on your orders and sent others to do the same. I buried my last shred of pride and never looked back. I did not betray this town."

Moon and I grabbed our pistols and holstered them.

"We know, Bett."

Part of her must've been relieved, but she hid it behind a new mask of outrage.

"You *know?* That's your answer? First, you malgados say I'm a traitor and ... what? Was this a test?"

"Apologies, my friend. We had to be sure."

"Everything I did for this town wasn't proof enough?"

"No," Moon said between puffs. "You did exactly what Raul accused you of. But you never realized it."

OK, Ixoca. Any time now would be great.

"Realized what? Give me a straight goddamn answer."

Moon nodded for me to resume the show.

"I'm afraid, my friend, you *were* planted here to spy on us."

"Bullshit, Raul."

"I'm sure you believe you traveled here of your own free will. But humans can easily fall prey to the power of suggestion. If there happens to be an angel of sorts whispering in your ear or speaking through your dreams ... well ... it's easy to believe the decisions are actually your own."

"Huh. You can't be serious."

I closed my pom and popped into her mind, where I tried to ease her toward the hard truth.

"A week after we returned from Todos Santos, you gave me your hand. I allowed a tiny essence of Ixoca to pass between us. At the time, you felt no change, or so you said. We established rules of contact to protect your personal privacy, as with all my lieutenants."

She pursed her lips and replied without words.

"You're trying to demonstrate how easy it is to control someone."

"Ilan and I can't control your actions, either through hypnosis or other programming. I suppose they'd be useful tools. But we happen to know someone who *can* manipulate your mind."

The hammer fell hard when Bett comprehended what we realized after hearing Cardinale's story. She didn't take it well.

"Ixoca? The Jewel of Eternity that's supposed to be our ally? The one you said we could trust."

I left her mind and spoke aloud.

"Trust is a moving target. But yes. Ixoca."

"It controlled my mind? Led me to Desperido? Used me to gather intel before you two merged with it? That's your conclusion."

The tension wasn't awkward at all.

"Ixoca has been moving pawns around for a thousand years. You're not the first."

Couldn't have been easy to realize she'd been played by a puppet master. Humans tended to fight any force that tried to squelch their free will, but most were blind to the strings.

"Bullshit. I'd have known if someone passed another piece of that – whatever the Jewel is – into my bloodstream."

A confident, disciplined voice entered the conversation. *Finally.*

"Perhaps I should explain," Ixoca whispered into my mind.

I held my irritation in check.

"Waiting for the perfect moment, were you?"

He pixelated red.

"Life is a journey of perfect moments, interspersed between tiresome gaps of lonely confusion."

"Truth, my friend." Moon also saw him. "Ixoca is with us, Bett. He wishes to explain his actions."

"The fuck? Where? What do you ...?"

I wagged a dismissive finger and retreated to internal dialogue.

"Reveal yourself, Ixoca. She needs to understand."

"You and Moon are the only ones able to see me."

"To quote Bett: Bullshit. Your repertoire extends far beyond what you disclosed. Show her, Ixoca. Tell her why you did it."

He morphed into his blended gender form.

"No human has seen my face since the Orpheus crashed. Not even my most important general."

"Shad Abdelmani. Your Q6 alter ego."

Ixoca nodded. I detected a twinge of embarrassment.

"Why, Ixoca? Do you believe they'll reject you?"

76

His naked, featureless form grew sandy hair. The skin shaded to a faint copper hue. The lips gained texture and shifted to a deep rose. The glowing blue irises lost their drama and settled into a simple Aztecan brown. Eyelashes and brows followed.

"I don't allow them to see me because they aren't worthy."

Spoken like a true god.

"Who are you becoming?"

"His name was Felipe Marzalos. The first Orpheus survivor who I saved from my own virus. He was a kind man. If not for him, I would have eliminated every human who set foot on Azteca."

"Ah. You want Bett to see you as a flesh-and-blood human."

"It should bridge the gap of understanding."

Yeah, no.

"Good luck with that, my friend. She's pissed, and Moon and I aren't exactly thrilled with your recent decisions."

OK, so that was putting it mildly. I walked a delicate line with this malgado. We weren't prepared to take him on head to head quite yet. And if we raised too many hackles ...

"The hell's going on?" Bett asked amid what must have seemed like a long, distracted silence.

"Ready?" I asked the Jewel, now clothed in the desert camouflage fatigues of Black Star. "I doubt she'll appreciate the gesture."

Ixoca stood across from Bett.

"Introduce me, Raul."

"I'm not your servant, Ixoca. Get it over with."

The Jewel/Felipe Marzalos responded with a mischievous little grin. Before I had time to worry what it meant, he saluted Bett.

"Reporting as ordered, Commander Ortiz."

Though I never proved it, Stopper might have pissed her pants.

9

I XOCA WASTED NO TIME creating the wrong impression. The Jewel walked *through* the table and extended a hand to Bett, who reached for her weapon. In fairness, Ixoca was socially awkward. The last time he showed himself to humans, he was trying to annihilate them.

Bett aimed her pistol.

"Not a step closer."

"Take care," I said. "You'll burn a hole into the wall, my friend."

Ixoca/Felipe retracted his hand.

"I apologize. Perhaps I came off too aggressive, Commander. How about if I take a seat in this empty chair? Then we can talk in a less threatening manner."

"The fuck we will."

"Settle, Bett. He's a projection."

She scoffed at the creature.

"This? This thing is Ixoca?"

"A piece of my heart from the distant past," the Jewel said. "Two such pieces live within you, Commander. The one Raul endowed, and the one I slipped inside you first. Will you allow me to explain my choices?"

Bett endured a rough morning. I wouldn't have blamed her for walking out. She saw Felipe, an average man forced to restart life on a desolate new world. Yet she heard Ixoca, who spoke with the patronizing arrogance of a so-called god. In her place, I wouldn't have trusted the first word out of anyone's mouth.

"What have you done to me, Ixoca?"

The Jewel slithered into a chair vacated by Sgt. Kato.

"Nothing of great consequence, Commander. You have not been physically altered. I penetrated your subconscious to gain a certain level of access."

"The fuck does that mean?"

Felipe pointed to the chair she abandoned.

"Please. Sit. For everyone's comfort."

Bett complied but did not holster her useless pistol. Was she following a command or acting of her own volition? Interesting.

"As Raul noted earlier, he and his partner came to my attention some time ago. I learned of their ambition through the eyes of my observer in this town, Lumen. But she was not an effective bridge between us. After the incident with your road train, I made contact with Raul and Ilan through my general, Horatio Vargas. I required an observer better suited to their ambition."

"So ... you what? Picked me out of a crowd of pigeons?"

"Many of my Children hold influential positions at Montez Shipping. Their eyes alerted me to your plight. One handshake was all it took to transfer a piece of me into you. The rest was suggestion. Entering your dreams. Softening you to the idea of a new life in Desperido."

She would've jumped the malgado if he were flesh and blood.

"You controlled me the whole time?"

Ixoca waved his hand.

"Not at all. I offered you an option. You chose it of your own accord. I counted on your anger and resentment to lead you here. I knew Raul and Ilan sought to build an army. You were the perfect liaison."

"Perfect mark, you mean."

"No, Commander. I left you alone for months. I commend your achievement and your leadership."

She scoffed at his praise. Who wouldn't?

"Tell me about last night."

Felipe/Ixoca pivoted to acknowledge everyone in the room.

"Raul and Ilan made a deal when we merged. I would provide resources to help build their empire, and they would do me a favor in return. Now, their empire – yours too, Commander – grows like wildflowers on fertile ground. The time for my favor has arrived."

I never presented the deal to Bett quite in those terms, but her anger with Ixoca exceeded any frustration with me. She laid her pistol on the table and leaned forward.

"The fuck does that have to do with last night?"

"It's not complicated, Commander. Black Star shifted its focus away from domestic concerns. Off-world success meant you would soon depart. I decided to readjust your focus ... for a brief time. Long enough for Black Star to repay its debt."

I didn't expect Ixoca to be forthcoming about his motives. Bett latched onto the bigger picture.

"You arranged an attack against us," she said, "but not bad enough to wipe us out."

"Correct. Many in government and the constabularies have wanted to act against Black Star. My Children provide a safety net. The cartels, however, were too distracted by their wars and oblivious to the underlying cause. I gave my top general, Shad Abdelmani, proof of Black Star's role. He did the rest."

"Lured them in by promising to wipe out Desperido."

"Yes. But I had one problem, for which I required an elegant solution. Your duty officers in the next room are outstanding, but none possess a piece of my heart."

"Meaning you can't control them."

Felipe nodded. "Had they been on duty, they would have seen the jump from Conquillos right away and activated missiles. They would have blasted that ship from the sky when it exited aperture. Its pieces would not have fallen onto Desperido."

Moon and I deduced his strategy hours ago and had time to cool our syneth. Not so for Bett, who pounded the table.

"You killed thirty of our people. Ten of my fighters. Warriors who fought for this planet!" She turned her rage toward Moon and me. "This is the asshole you told us to trust?"

"The same, Bett."

"You two knew all along it wasn't me."

What could I do but sigh and concede the embarrassing truth?

"We assumed, but we needed certainty, my friend. We had hoped to draw out Ixoca sooner and elicit a confession. He played the role of a cagey malgado. Yes?"

Felipe shrugged and rose from his chair.

"I must admit, events did not unfold as I predicted. The Salazar boy's survival and your subsequent assault on Cardinale's stronghold allowed you access to information I never intended to reveal."

Now I was a touch more pissed.

"Devilish bastard. You wanted us angry enough to seek vengeance against our enemies."

Felipe crossed his so-called arms and pursed his lips.

"Similar to Bett, I counted on rage and grief to motivate Black Star. The task before your people will be grim. I need you in the proper frame of mind. The funeral proved I succeeded."

Moon spoke for me when he said:

"You feared we'd back out of our promise to finish what we started. You can't complete the next operation without our soldiers."

"Yes, Ilan. But you've known that for some time."

Bett interjected. "What's he talking about?"

I resumed the interchange.

"Weeks ago, Ixoca said the entire Children of Orpheus would be summoned to one location. He never explained why. He also said Black Star would be there. Yesterday, he told me final preparations had been made for this so-called reunion. I asked how many fighters he'd require. He said sixty or seventy. We were attacked hours later."

Bett massaged her temples.

"I need a drink. Just so I understand, Raul. You promised troops for whatever he's planning, but he came down on us anyway."

Ixoca beat me to the punch.

"Yes, Commander. Arrangements had been made. Participants assured of the town's destruction. If I ordered Abdelmani to abort the mission, he would've lost face. And your enemies – three cartels worth – would have found other ways to attack this town and enlist more allies. You may detest my decision ..."

"That's a goddamn understatement, you murdering cunt ..."

"... but there is far more at stake than the loss of a few dozen lives. I had to ensure my interests were preserved and motivated to act on my behalf."

That sounded about right. Even made good sense. Hell, I'd been putting my own needs ahead of everyone most of my lives. We gods focused on macro concerns. Still, I couldn't let this stand.

"In another context, my friend, Ilan and I might have supported your decision. We've often left behind heavy collateral losses in the vicinity of our targets."

He nodded. "As you did last night at Cardinale's ranch."

"Indeed. But your actions amounted to a betrayal of trust. If you were human, you'd be dead by now – likely at her hands. We can't harm you." So far as the lunatic knew. "You could have voiced your concerns at any time. We've been faithful partners from the outset. We remained so even after learning the truth about the fort. Which brings me to the essential question: Why should Black Star not leave this planet today?"

I knew the answer, of course, but I needed Bett to hear it. We had all but lost her.

"It's true," Felipe said. "I can't stop you. And I would never kill my fellow gods." I wanted to call bullshit but held my tongue. "Yet I know everything about Black Star. Even now, my many eyes extend to Bolivar and Indonesia Prime. Soon, I will have Genoa's eyes inside your Inuit facility. With the help of my generals, I could wreak havoc on your empire. I could live inside the dreams of your lieutenants and convince them to turn against you."

Ixoca cut himself off with a condescending grin.

"Not to worry. I'd never resort to such betrayal. Weeks ago, I told you the arrow points in one direction but must be guided by a steady hand. My actions might have stretched the metaphor."

"What a lovely euphemism," I said, pivoting to Bett. "Ilan and I made a deal beneath Todos Santos. We won't be free of Ixoca's presence until we conclude our deal. Black Star must accommodate. Stopper, you command our forces. We don't intend that to change, unless you have other ideas."

I didn't envy the woman. Thirty minutes ago, we called her a traitor. Now we asked her to lead our army into battle.

Life. What a spicy stew.

Bett likely needed more than one drink. She balled her fists and reared back as if prepared to punch the wall. She thought better of a useless gesture.

"Ixoca, you'll stay inside my head until the day I die. Right?"

"As long as you're useful, Commander. Yes. There will never be pain, and I believe you might actually live longer."

"I'd blow my brains out before that happens. The only way to get rid of you is to finish this favor. Right?"

"Correct."

"Then I'll do it. Whatever the fuck it takes." She leered at us. "Then we go our separate ways. Deal?"

Two fallen gods and a Jewel of Eternity nodded in unison. For a moment, a human had leverage over all three. How about that?

"One condition," she added. "I want to know the mission. Here and now. No more screwing around."

Ixoca hit us with the side-eye, to which I shrugged.

"She's right, my friend. You've led us down this winding path for too long. If the arrangements have been made, as you say, what's left to hold back? Where and when are we to join the Children of Orpheus? And what precisely do you expect from us?"

The Jewel no doubt enjoyed dangling his favor in front of us for months. I suspect Felipe's frown reflected his sadness at having to surrender the secret at long last.

Frank Kennedy – White Sunset

10

"A FEW DAYS AHEAD OF SCHEDULE makes no difference," Ixoca said after pondering our demand. "Raul, open your pom. Retrieve your topographical surveys of Ixtapa. The ones you generated from your first study of Founders Memorial."

Huh. I instructed Bart to compile those during the early days in Desperido, while I conducted research on Lumen, the Children of Orpheus, and that damn gear tattoo on Vash and his assassins.

"How did you know about ...? Ah. I see! Never mind."

It all fit together.

I presented Lumen with my findings in order to enhance my leverage. Lumen, the Jewel's passive observer.

Days later, our fort was destroyed. Eh.

The holos expanded to feature several angles of the Ixtapa coastal region, stretching from the sandy shore where Orpheus crashed – now Founders Memorial – to a narrow range of dormant volcanic mountains ten kilometers inland.

"My Children will come together at Ixtapa. A fitting reunion."

"Ah. The place where it all began. Big on symmetry, are you?"

"This region is sacred. Everyone who will attend bears the genetic stamp of an Orpheus survivor."

"How many?" Moon asked.

Felipe beamed like a proud father.

"Eight hundred and seventeen."

Moon undercut his joy.

"That's all? Should've been bigger after eleven hundred years."

The Jewel bowed his head and sighed.

"Yes. I might have expected at least tens of thousands from the original five hundred. Alas, many family lines ended in the first century. Azteca proved challenging for early generations of settlers, similar to other colonies. Some abandoned the faith. To the positive: These people represent hardy genetic stock. A millennium of change never shook their ancestral belief in me or a greater destiny for Aztecans."

"Sounds like a fucking cult," Bett said, hands on hips.

I reached the same conclusion from day one. Felipe scoffed.

"My cult, as you erroneously call it, includes many of the most influential, intellectual, and committed minds on this planet. They control most of the critical levers of power. Those who do not, like the former owner of your cantina, remain devout."

"Interesting, my friend. Lumen will be attending?"

"Oh, yes. She reunited with her grandchildren. She will attend along with them and her late son's widow."

The son we incinerated. That reunion wouldn't be awkward at all.

"What of the thousands who possess a piece of you but are not descended from Orpheus?"

"Unimportant, Raul. Their eyes provide passive intelligence and allow me into the halls of power off world. Few are Aztecan."

"Slow down," Bett said. "I'm confused. If those people aren't Aztecan, how do you see through their eyes?"

Felipe grinned. "It was a very slow process. Some visited Azteca on business, military, or government interests. One of my Children made their acquaintance. A simple handshake did the rest. Others met power brokers during their travels. For example, I sent one to Amity Station last year in hopes of infiltrating the President. He failed, but he met the President's Chief of Staff. Close enough."

The Jewel's extra detail about Kai Parke felt like a veiled threat to reveal our connection to the Prez. Of course, he'd deny it.

"We've tilted off course," I said. "Back to Ixtapa, please. Where and when will your Children meet?"

"Not where you might think."

Ixoca pointed toward a section of the inland mountains.

"There. Zoom in on that specific cluster."

We stared at three craggy peaks surrounding a lush valley two kilometers wide.

"Lovely, my friend. Mountains and forest. No structures. Will these influential, intellectual, and committed Aztecans pitch tents?"

Felipe laughed. "I love your sense of humor, Raul. You know me better than that."

Moon beat me to the punch.

"It's cloaked. Just like Desperido."

"Very good, Ilan. It uses the same technology I provided you to construct the oasis dome."

"Why hide it?" Bett asked.

Felipe took umbrage. "Why hide Desperido? The structure my Children spent decades building was vulnerable. If the wrong eyes recognized it, the project would have collapsed."

"Interesting, my friend. Months ago, my research stumbled upon a series of designs being passed around by industrial contractors who I now realize were your Children. Each design appeared to be infrastructure for something grand in scale, but I never learned the shape of it. Lumen spent years siphoning town profits toward the Children of Orpheus, as did other members. The credits went toward this project. Yes?"

Felipe applauded.

"A mystery solved, Raul. I was surprised when you didn't pursue the evidence further."

"Difficult, Ixoca. Your people are very good at erasing evidence from data spools and the global stream."

"Indeed they are."

"What's beneath the cloak?" Bett demanded.

"Many lifetimes of work, Commander. The fulfillment of a dream.

You'll understand when you pass through the dome. My Children will arrive in twelve days. Your army will arrive in eleven. Two of my trusted generals will greet you. Horatio Vargas and Martin Jimenez."

That tidbit raised all our hackles.

"Jimenez?" Bett said. "That asshole?"

The former governor of Monteria Province, who we forced to resign at Conquillos Base when we threatened to kill his family, had kept a surprisingly low profile in the following weeks. He was ringleader of the anti-Collectorate movement, a direct descendant of an Orpheus survivor, and had his hand in countless pockets.

"Can't imagine he'll be pleased to see us, my friend."

"You'll be surprised, Raul. Martin is an ambitious man and yes, you humiliated him. But he's had time to understand the complexity of our arrangement. We have a fine working relationship, and he knows your importance to me."

"Huh. Sounds very tidy, Ixoca. This is why you insisted we not kill him at Conquillos."

Felipe responded with a sheepish grin.

"Martin made an important professional sacrifice that day. His life was too much to ask. I gave up Anton Cherry and Maris Sylva, though they were both my Children. I accommodated your needs in the spirit of our alliance."

"As I recall, Ixoca, you expressed personal disdain for Senor Cherry and Senora Sylva. You said they had behaved poorly as generals."

He winked when I caught him in a convenient memory lapse.

"True, Raul. They *were* reprehensible malgados."

"Nope," Bett said. "That ain't good enough for me. Jimenez deserves a bolt between the eyes. He and his lot ruined thousands of veterans' lives. They're working to overthrow the government and break away from the Collectorate. They'll start a goddamn civil war."

"From a certain point of view, yes," Felipe replied. "He and his kind pose a paramount threat to Aztecans who wish to remain inside the Collectorate. And yes, Martin saw veterans as a threat. Most of my

Children in positions of influence followed his lead; Anton and Maris among the worst offenders. But Martin is a politician. He is more flexible on these matters. You'll be amenable when you hear the entire plan."

Bett held her ground, hands still planted on hips.

"He's a dead man, Ixoca." She saved her wrath for me. "I sold my fighters on a crusade to take down these assholes. You expect me to go out there and tell them to play nice with the fucks who ruined their lives and dishonored their sacrifice?"

Felipe interjected: "Black Star thrives because my Children have shielded you. Ask yourself why."

"Already did. No answer. We're enemies."

"Both groups have something in common. Without me, neither one thrives. With all due apologies to your hard work and sacrifice, of course."

Bett responded with another rant, but I didn't pay it any mind. Instead, I zeroed in on Ixoca's tone, which raised the bar on arrogance and overconfidence. The clues built over many months took form. I shoved square pegs into round holes.

Ah. Nothing quite topped a moment of revelation.

"Silence, Bett," I said. "You miss his point. The Jewel created a crucible by design. After his Children arrive at Ixtapa, they'll go public with their plans for Azteca. They'll announce a 'great new destiny,' or something to that effect. They'll reveal Ixoca's existence and his role in sculpting the planet, perhaps even unveil his three thousand terraform shafts. Sound about right, Ixoca?"

Felipe bowed. "Well done."

"Except words won't work on their own. Most people would perceive them as the rantings of lunatics. Or a garden-variety cult. They need a powerful symbol. Something to stir emotions." I pointed to the lush valley. "Something large. Say, about two kilometers long. Something every Aztecan will recognize from their history texts."

Moon's eyes lit up. Bett followed soon after, her jaw limp.

"The fuck, you say?"

I satisfied Felipe's shit-eating grin.

"Designs for heat induction, habitat modules, water reclamation units, banquet halls, a city park. I never put them together because I was thinking in terrestrial terms. I forgot about the ancient city-ships that ferried billions of humans to their new homes."

Moon laughed. "You built an Ark Carrier in that valley."

"I'll take a guess," Bett added. "You call it Orpheus."

"Oh, Commander. Not just calling it by that name. It *is* the Orpheus. Down to the square meter, a perfect replica. I salvaged some of her skeleton from the original crash. What I destroyed then, I reconstituted for this re-creation."

"I am impressed, my friend. Of all the possibilities, that one never crossed my mind. Is it space-worthy?"

"Oh, yes."

"Should be quite a show. Will make headlines throughout the Collectorate. Might even inspire many Aztecans who thought little about independence. Yet it won't be enough. Will it?"

Felipe's long, baleful sigh admitted I was one step ahead.

"You're right, Raul. My analysis of the Aztecan people says they're too indifferent. They were slow to rise against the Chancellors or the Swarm. They will not fight en masse until they are enraged. They must believe in more than the rightness of independence. We must light a fire in their bellies."

Moon got it.

"You have to generate an enemy."

I added, "A brutal, oppressive force so deadly it will stop at nothing to end the separatist movement. Only one such force exists."

Bett cursed under her breath.

"The UNF. You've been laying the groundwork for months."

"My Children. Yes. But also Black Star. Your missions to Conquillos Base have generated mistrust and paranoia. What happens next will paint an undeniable picture: The enemy exists not just among the stars but also close to home. Aztecans will take up arms to fight the Collectorate and any neighbor who supports it."

Bett's early rage softened to stunned disbelief.

"Civil war. You wanted this all along."

"What I want is for Aztecans to achieve their destiny. The method is irrelevant."

"The fuck it is. I ..."

"Bett. Stop. Ixoca, my friend. How will this work?"

"Black Star will pose as security for my Children. Horatio and Martin agreed to these terms. The Orpheus will leave its moorings. My Children will broadcast their message of revelation from high above Ixtapa. Orpheus will then be flown into orbit. The enemy will reveal itself on two fronts.

"First, Black Star will forcibly take command of Orpheus. You will execute most of my Children's leadership. You will send a message stating your allegiance to the Collectorate. Soon thereafter, a UNF warship will exit aperture. It will call for Orpheus to stand down. Black Star will leave by shuttle and rendezvous with the warship.

"Moments later, that warship will fire one particle missile and destroy the Orpheus. The warship will leave the Aztecan system, and Black Star will be free to pursue its own destiny."

OK then. Not too far from the sequence I predicted. The warship was a nice wrinkle. One bit was a blatant lie, but no need to dwell on it at the moment. I had to give Ixoca some credit: This malgado did not believe in half measures.

Bett rose from the awkward silence first.

"I ... I don't even know what to say. Y-you spent centuries inside people's heads talking about some great goddamn destiny. You spend years and fuck-all how much money rebuilding the Orpheus. And just like that, you kill them? You blow up the ship? You're mad. What in ten hells did I get my mates into?"

"A place in history," Felipe said with crystal clear pride. "Is that not part and parcel to Black Star's goals? Disorder. Chaos. Murder."

"We'll be the enemy. We'll never be able to come home again. And your so-called Children will be martyrs."

"Yes. And yes."

Moon and I couldn't help but smile. The sheer scope of it truly belonged in the God Wannabe Hall of Fame.

"What do you think, partner?" I asked him. "Winning plan?"

A smoke cloud hovered above Moon.

"Doable." He eyed the Jewel. "You'll separate from us?"

"I will," Ixoca said. "First, you will reabsorb the pieces you planted in your lieutenants. You two will briefly return to Todos Santos, where we will decouple. Our business will be at an end."

Moon shrugged. "Good enough, so long as you keep your word."

My partner knew how to play this game; Moon realized much of what we'd just been presented was utter bullshit. Still, I wanted to fill in a few gaps without raising the Jewel's suspicions.

"That warship, Ixoca. I assume it is a decommissioned vessel which will be disguised otherwise."

He nodded. "The UNF's denials will fall on deaf ears."

"And the captain of its skeleton crew? Someone you know, I presume? Shad Abdelmani?"

"Indeed. And yes, Raul. To the other question swirling in your mind: Shad *was* the Captain you saw who ordered your fort destroyed. I lied weeks ago when I said he died. I simply eliminated his many eyes from your view. My apologies for the necessary deception."

Moon didn't seem terribly bothered, nor was I. We knew Ixoca played many games from the outset. He'd been refining his art for thousands of years.

"You had your reasons, Ixoca. I won't legislate the past. But I would ask one favor."

"By all means, Raul."

"If you're willing to close so many of your eyes, you won't be bothered if I kill Abdelmani."

He frowned. "He is my most valuable off-world agent. Seems like a waste. But, if you consider him a worthy prize, who am I to object? Fulfill your mission, and he's yours."

"Lovely. We appreciate your forthrightness, my friend. And for showing yourself to Bett. Now, if you don't mind, we have a great deal to process and fortunately, several days in which to do it. Any parting words, Stopper?"

She had fallen into her chair, the color gone from her cheeks. Not the best day. When she said nothing, Felipe saluted everyone.

"Working with you continues to be a joy. I look forward to our final operation together. Now, I must attend to other business."

He vanished in a snap, but he'd be listening with the heart of a paranoid lunatic. I focused on quelling the immediate problem. I sat beside Bett and adjusted my tone to pillow-soft sweetness.

"I don't recall a day that began with such a buffet of revelation, my friend. Much of it shocked us as well. Before you make any decisions, Bett, I hope you'll focus on what this means for our nine hundred contractors and soldiers. They committed to a new life, and all have been rewarded with wealth beyond their aspirations. They can start anew. Experience lives of adventure and great comfort. If we do not fulfill Ixoca's request – no matter how extreme it may be – all their futures will be in doubt."

I gave her a moment to reflect, and she gave me a middle finger.

Huh. I saw that gesture in a few other universes, but not Alpha.

"Miserable fucks, both of you."

"True, but you knew that from day one. You are like us, Stopper. You're a killer. It's in your heart. And on the brightest side: You will personally oversee the deaths of all the assholes who ruined your livelihood and dishonored your service. Yes, a torrent of blood will flow, but justice will be earned."

I left her side and nodded for Moon to follow. I cracked open the door and said:

"We'll leave you here to think. Call out to me when you reach the proper decision."

She stifled a laugh.

"If I reach the *improper* decision, you'll kill me."

I was in no position to explain myself, not with Ixoca listening. So I settled on a hard truth.

Frank Kennedy – White Sunset

"I know of no other punishment for a traitor."

11

BETT KEPT A HEALTHY DISTANCE the next few days. Outside of logistical meetings, she hid inside Mod 1 and fraternized with her mates. Moon and I took no offense. We maintained a full agenda. Clearing out Desperido proved more complicated than expected.

Many of the long-timers simply did not want to leave. In great part, they'd lost sight of a future beyond this desert enclave. I thought the attack on our town would've illustrated a basic tenet: One cannot hide from proper society forever. It will come for you, perhaps in the form of fireballs. Best to run!

Eh. The indecisive hundred — those who did not commit to resuming their lives with Black Star — we saved for last. All other civilians prepared for new lives in faraway systems. Many required retraining. The skills they brought to Desperido did not often translate to our operations on Inuit, Bolivar, G'hladi, or Indy Prime.

The first evacuations began one day after Elian and his team submitted their final report. Twenty-five gathered outside Scramjet Maria. Destination: G'hladi.

We encouraged them to travel light and think of the journey as a rebirth. We allowed two parcels each: A satchel for limited wardrobe and one case containing personal valuables. The artists pitched a hissy-fit, insisting they bring along their entire collections. After receiving a hard "no," we offered them alternative destinations, each

95

progressively more uncomfortable. Usually, a reminder that their bank accounts would greet them on a new world proved a sufficient motivator.

Ah, those bank accounts. Universal Credit Vouchers. I had to give the People's Collectorate their due; establishing a single interstellar currency offered their best hope at stability. The fools who wanted independence had no idea what financial separation would do to their economies. I knew full well and couldn't wait for the day. Black Star would flourish on self-inflicted misfortune.

Not every civilian gave two shits about the money. I discovered as much while walking among the first group of evacuees.

I approached a care worker with whom I hadn't spoken since an incident in the Circle many weeks ago. His courage that night helped seal unity between the military and civilians.

Diego, a svelte man in his mid-thirties who made his pain public in an elegant speech, wore a full-length smock and slung a bag over his shoulder. He'd grown a beard since he talked to the Circle.

"Is this all you intend to carry with you, my friend?" I asked.

Diego shot back with a toothy grin.

"I came to Desperido with less."

"Ah. Yes. A minimalist. You defy the trend."

"Never had much choice. I was always on the run or barely had a credit to my name."

Judging from his simple attire, Diego did not use his deepened bank account to improve his lot.

"Think differently on G'hladi. Their bazaars are legendary, and they've resumed in the Smirnash District now that our facility is bringing new prosperity. Not to mention, your clientele might expect a different fashion sense."

Diego shadowed his eyes.

"I'm leaving that career behind, boss. I intend to learn a trade."

"Ah. Any ideas?"

"Not sure. I'm good with my hands. Construction? Everyone says we'll be raising a small city over the dead poltash fields. I used a phasic drill on a job maybe fifteen years ago." He laughed at the thought. "And I need to get more sun."

"You *are* pale, not unlike most of Desperido's mole people. Also, be prepared to buy something heavier when you arrive. It's winter there, and they actually have seasons."

Diego imitated a shiver. "I hear they'll be expecting snow in a few days. Never seen snow, but it has to be an improvement on the dust."

I recalled the aftermath of a battle with the Swarm where bodies formed lumps beneath new-fallen snow.

"Context is everything, Diego. All the best on your new adventure."

I tipped my hat and started away, but Diego left his place in line to saunter alongside.

"Raul. Boss. I ... uh ... I never had a chance to properly thank you."

"For what, my friend?"

"Sticking up for us during our troubles."

I tipped my hat again, thinking he'd get the point.

"A service I was happy to provide, Diego. Now if ..."

"But you see, boss. That's just it. We didn't actually want your help. To be honest, we just assumed you didn't give a shit about us. We saw how you ran off Lumen. Then you brought in this army, and ... we knew you and Ilan did horrible things to people. When Saul gathered us together, we thought you'd send us packing. Or worse."

He shuffled his feet and glanced toward Maria, understandably ashamed by his confession.

"I'm glad we were wrong about you, boss."

I wasn't sure why he chose to unburden himself now.

"Diego, I'm not much of a teacher. Being a god, I don't have many relatable lessons to share. Take this with you, for what it's worth: Everyone is misunderstood. No exceptions. Even ravenous killers like my partner and I can summon the occasional soft touch. Yes?"

The anxiety wrinkles above his brow disappeared.

"I won't forget. Oh, and one last thing. I heard you plan to destroy the town after everyone leaves. Is that true?"

"It will be a hole in the desert. Are you disappointed?"

He chuckled. "This place? We never lived here. We just survived."

Diego wasn't wrong, but he also missed the point.

"It sustained you until opportunity walked into the cantina. That's no small feat for the middle of nowhere."

"True, boss. Last thing, and I'll let you go. Now that we're gonna be scattered across the sector, how often should we plan to see you and Ilan?"

A loaded question, indeed. Diego did not need to know the truth.

"We'll always be a wormhole away. Count on us when you least expect us."

Diego extended his hand.

"Look forward to the day, boss. Thank you for everything."

"You are most welcome, Diego. They're loading now. You should hurry. Farewell."

Nice fella. Couldn't imagine him on a construction crew.

A few others glanced back at Desperido before they boarded, but they weren't stupid. Their pockets were fat; they and Azteca parted ways long ago. Sentiment did not win the day.

Wasn't certain how I'd feel when the evacuation began. In the early days, I never anticipated a peaceful migration for these folks. Most, I assumed, would die forgotten in this gorgeous wasteland.

Yet everyone on the first flight out stopped briefly by the cantina en route to the Scramjet. They glanced through the gaping hole and took a moment to reflect. Through everything, the cantina offered solace and community.

I gave Lumen credit. She kept it sparkling, far more than the town ever deserved. The folks who took charge afterward did their best, but it was never the same.

Huh. Would've been nice if we had the honor of decimating it ourselves rather than the enemy.

I walked inside, broken glass crunching beneath my boots. The closest half was charred. Six died instantly when a section of the attacker's portside hull crashed through the wall. One was Saul, severed through his gut. What furniture survived lay toppled like leftover construction debris. Oddly enough, the liquor fared better than the humans. More than half the display shelves Lumen curated remained intact. The bottles became collectors' items after the last bodies were removed.

To be fair, our little town served high-class brands. Only the best for our local looters.

I leaped across the bar and found half a bottle of green liquor. Not my preferred, but it would do. All I needed were a pair of shot glasses and ... there they were! I was soon in business.

I popped into Ship's mind.

"Change of venue, my friend. Meet me in the bar."

Bett, Moon, and I were paring down the roster of troops to join us at Ixtapa, roughly half of the hundred twenty still based in town. Ship grew impatient to know his role. My vague responses led the kid to suspect I'd transfer him for his own good. Time to settle affairs.

A moment later, he stood silhouetted in the sunlight.

"Boss? You in there?"

"Please, Ship. Join me for a drink."

He walked gingerly, as if he might step on an overlooked body part.

"Never thought I'd walk inside this place again. Why here, boss?"

I opened the bottle and poured.

"Pull up a stool, my friend. I'll serve *you* for a change."

I found a rag and wiped considerable dust off the counter. Ship did the same with his stool. I handed him a full glass and held up my own.

"Do you remember your first day in Lumen's employ?"

He cracked a smile. "I was scared shitless. I dropped my tray twice."

"Look how far you've come, my friend. Cheers."

We drank together. Ship clenched his teeth to gird against the liquor's not-so-subtle heat.

"All thanks to you, boss."

"To some degree. You haven't forgotten Lumen's role in literally saving your life."

He sighed like he didn't want to be reminded.

"It's hard, boss. Yeah, she saved me from being spaced. Then she treated me like an indentured servant for the next five years."

"Everyone has their price, Ship. Payment often comes with pain. Sometimes, pain *is* the payment. If you're to be my enforcer, you'll not only embrace that principle, you'll exact it upon our enemies."

Ship grabbed the bottle and poured another.

"Anything and everything. I'm ready."

He threw back a second shot. I did not join him.

"No. You're not. But that's OK. My tutelage will take you the distance. However, you are well positioned, seeing as you're already a mass murderer. You killed far more assholes in six months than I did in the equivalent. Of course, I lacked a master teacher."

"I'm a lucky man."

"Not lucky. Blessed. I have many plans for you, but none can begin until we've finished our business on Azteca."

He leaned forward and ballooned those big, bright eyes.

"You made a decision about my role?"

"It's all a bit fluid until we arrive on the Orpheus. Suffice to say, you will not be pulling up the rear."

"Thanks, boss. I was afraid you ..."

I waved him quiet. "An irrational fear, Ship. Relegating you from our most important mission to date would speak poorly to my faith in your ability. Yes?"

Ship rapped the counter.

"Actually, boss, I've spent the last few days thinking about the future at your side. I still have a long way to go, many skillsets to hone. I need to prove just how far I can go in your service."

"Meaning?"

"What I did at Everdeen showed I can kill without mercy. I

murdered my mother and brother and felt nothing for them. Never lost a minute of sleep. That Cardinale kid I popped? It was easy. Fun. Business. I never gave two fucks about him. Anyone you need dead, I'm your man. But that ain't enough by a long shot, is it?"

My protégé passed his first exam with flying colors.

"Correct, Ship. Assassins are easy hires. I could build an army of them. But most lack certain traits. As a result, they'll never ascend to management. What are the traits they – and you – lack?"

Ship's placid half-smile said he knew the answer before I asked the question. He'd been studying texts on the criminal mind.

"Elegance," he said. "Sophistication. Superior language skills."

"Good. And the big one?"

"A goal, boss."

I poured a second shot and toasted him.

"Nice, my friend. Sounds simple, yes? Emulate me, and you'll have it all figured out."

"Nope. I can't be you. I made that mistake for months. I thought if I tried to follow in your footsteps ..."

We shared an ironic laugh.

"I spent centuries honing this unparalleled magnificence because that's what time afforded me. You lack the luxury. But if you're to become feared, respected, and mentioned in the same breath as me, you'll have to adapt on an accelerated timeline. Won't be easy."

"No worries, boss. I'm up to the task."

He had no idea.

"At times, you will serve as my proxy. I will expect you to carry out monstrous acts against our enemies but also those caught in the middle, to whom we must make a point. The red tide will rise in your wake, my friend, but you will do so with a smile and a well-timed *bon mot*. More to the point: Develop a sense of humor. Play games with them. Toy with their minds and mold them to your preference. If you cannot command the room, you will fail."

Ship nodded with certainty.

"I haven't been assertive in the meetings. I spend so much time watching you and Ilan play off each other, I forget to make a strong contribution."

"Don't beat yourself up. There is wisdom in knowing when to keep your mouth shut. A chatterbox who speaks in empty verse tends to have a limited shelf life. No. Speak when you can contribute, not simply to be heard. That would be Elian's primary flaw."

Ship rolled his eyes.

"He doesn't know when to zip it shut."

"True. I thought Indy Prime would settle that tendency. Oh, well. I'm neither flawless nor a soothsayer. But Elian's legacy is secured, no matter how he conducts himself. In time, someone will cut him off with a well-aimed laser bolt. That's no concern of yours.

"Ship, if you're to stand at my side, build your own brand. You'll measure success by how far-ranging your reputation of animus and atrocity extends. If enemies across the sector are gunning for you, and each day stands even-odds to be your last, then you have eclipsed the ordinary and become the creature I need."

I saw a darkness lurk in Ship's eyes – or perhaps it was merely the dim, ambient lighting.

"A well-dressed, well-spoken monster," he said.

I threw back another shot.

"Succinct, my friend. Our goal is nothing less than to knock the pins out from underneath civilization. When we're free of Azteca, every act must serve that future. Objective observers would call us evil men. They would not be wrong. Evil disguised in the trappings of elegant beauty is all but impossible to contain. Ship, do you consider yourself an evil man?"

He stared at the bottle, now less than a quarter full. Did he want to want answer honestly or to suit my ears?

"I'm angry and vengeful. I feel my blood stirring, boss. No. I'm not evil."

"You've hit upon your goal, my friend." I pointed to a spot ten feet away. "I sat there almost eight months ago and asked Lumen to fill five shot glasses. Fifteen minutes later, this town belonged to me.

From that day, she knew what I was, and her best efforts to stop me failed. She knew this town would die with me at the helm.

"She was right, but how many Desperidans followed her on Roadway 9? How many preferred to stick with our little journey into the abyss? Even now, most of those who've chosen not to continue with Black Star are older and tired. The rest want more, no matter what it takes – or how many stars they must cross to grab it. In a few days, Desperido will be a memory. One pin down. Millions more to go. Does that prospect excite you, Ship?"

He hopped off the stool, walked to the spot where I changed history, and rubbed the counter as if it were sacred.

"Hell yes."

The darkness in his eyes was real, after all. Birthing, perhaps, but certain to grow.

"That's how it always begins, my friend. Before long, it spreads faster than humans can hope to control. We proved it, Moon and I. We changed the course of life in all nine universes. Reshaped reality. Killed billions of people. That's billions with a *b*."

He met my smile with a frozen stare. At first, I sensed terror. Just as quickly, it morphed into revelation. Then wonder.

"Moon," he said deadpan. "Moon is ...?"

"Ilan's true name. Mine is Royal. We were human until twenty years ago in Collectorate Standard Time. We died. We evolved outside time itself. We learned, we ascended, we conquered, and we escaped." I chuckled. "Then we returned and had endless fun. We saw the first light and the last. We destroyed whole planets and ended the Swarm war. We triggered The Wave. We fought the original head beast. *Father and Mother.* The only god stronger than us.

"Now we begin again. And you, my friend, are the only human in Creation who knows our truth. I trust you feel honored."

He didn't faint. Nice start. It was a bit much for a boy of seventeen to digest, but the timing felt right.

"It's ... it's all true, isn't it? I always wondered if I'd ever learn what you actually were. This ... I ..."

I poured another drink.

"Here. You need this."

He tossed it back like water and grabbed the bottle.

"I want to know everything, boss."

"In time."

"Should I call you Royal?"

"No. That's privileged information."

"Why tell me now?"

"I had planned to wait until after Azteca. But one of the care workers made an insightful observation. Soon, we'll be scattered across the sector. Even with a worm drive, I can't be everywhere at once. Nor Moon. That means our top generals will act on our behalf in many systems.

"Ship, I will need you to be my sword, my gun, my exterminator. Where you walk, I walk. Anything shy of that standard will be unacceptable. Do you take my meaning?"

He polished off the next shot.

"I do."

"Your life is mine, Ship. From the moment you gave me access to this town, you became mine. Every word, every deed will reflect upon me until the final, agonizing breath you take. The reward for a job well done? When they build a statue to Royal and Moon, you will stand at our side. The punishment for failure? I'll incinerate you alive and no one will ever mention the name Ship Foster.

"I told you everyone has a price. This is mine. Accept it, and we go forward. Reject it, and I'll save you the trouble of a long life. What will it be, my dear friend?"

As I watched him quiver between excitement and terror, I wondered if he realized my deal wasn't much better than Lumen's. He was still an indentured servant, moving from one master to the next. Except no one would ever rescue him from me.

What a moment! I felt sparks ignite my syneth.

Was I right about him from the first day?

Ship raised his prosthetic arm and saluted.
Yes. He owed me for life, and he damn well knew it.
"Always, boss. Until the day I die."
Monsters weren't hard to come by. Loyal ones were rare.

12

MOON WAITED OUTSIDE OUR BUNKER, arms crossed and surrounded by the usual smoke cloud. Under normal circumstance, I might have attributed his foul demeanor to the latest logistical briefing, which he attended without me. Bett seemed to carry less of an aversion to him, but she made herself clear through internal dialogue: After the Ixtapa mission, she was done with both of us.

His animus, however, had nothing to do with the evacuation timetable or duty roster for Ixtapa. To be fair, he had every right to lay into me. I took the next step without consulting him.

"Watched the entire show, my friend?"

He blew smoke in my face.

"We agreed. No one but Ixoca."

"Our secret is safe with Ship. I needed to know the depth of his commitment."

"If he fell short?"

"You know the punishment, Moon." I swept past him downstairs. "No one would've seen or heard of Ship Foster again."

He followed, of course. For an instant, I thought he might lunge and throw a fist.

"Every time you violate your own edicts, Royal, your credibility takes a hit."

"With whom? You?"

"Asshole. I advised against pushing Stopper too hard. I thought you agreed. But you went ahead with it."

"I felt no pushback from you, my friend. You turned the show over to me, so I chewed the scenery. You know my style."

He pointed in my face, a somewhat churlish and childish move, frankly. Did two thousand years not teach him how to massage my ego during an argument?

"We almost lost her support."

"The Jewel played along, and we're moving forward. Bett won't be important after Ixtapa. Ship, on the other hand, has been my project from day one. I still believe he can become the most feared human being in the forty systems. It will take years. Yes. But he can't meet his potential until he knows everything."

"Today was not the time."

I reached for my favorite whiskey.

"I disagree. For what it's worth, I didn't expect to go there so soon. It happened in the spur of the moment."

"Trusting a human with that information ..."

"In Ship's case, there's no danger." I decided to equivocate. "Elian, on the other hand, wouldn't be able to bottle the truth for a week. Yet we owe him far more than Ship. Agree, partner?"

Those two hadn't been as close since Indonesia Prime. Moon vowed to detach himself. He succeeded for the most part, but I knew he'd ache to bring Elian into the closest of circles.

"I'll concede the point, Royal. Any other surprises in the offing?"

I pretended to review my timetable.

"No, my friend. Five days to finish the evacuation. Eight days to Ixtapa. Soon after, we bid farewell to the Jewel and lay siege to the People's Collectorate."

There were other surprises, of course, but Ixoca need not be made aware. Moon played along until he didn't.

"During the course of your heart to heart with Ship, were you paying attention to the other eyes?"

"From the periphery, but I wasn't listening. What did I miss?"

"The President made a decision about Riyadh."

Well, shit. And I'd kept such good tabs on her office.

"Tell me."

"She arranged a state visit to Riyadh City on Standard Day 119. She and the Emir will meet that evening."

Now, that qualified as an eyebrow-raiser.

"Ah. We know when she'll die. That's two SDs after Orpheus."

"We'll be free of Azteca, partner. There won't be a goddamn thing holding us back."

I saw his gears working. Always a dangerous proposition.

"You still want us to consider the possibility for interfering."

"Not for her sake. I don't give ten hells what happens to her. But if we save her from sure death, she'll have to acknowledge us. We might even be able to talk her into disclosing what happened twenty years ago. If the human race knows the truth ..."

"They'll bother us for autographs. Or worse."

Moon didn't appreciate my snark.

"It won't slow the work. We'll have our run of the place."

"True, my friend. But it will also screw with the timeline. If she lives, there's every possibility the Collectorate stays in one piece for many years. That will not work to our advantage."

Moon and I dug into this debate before. It never went anywhere.

"She has many enemies, Royal. Saving her might be the very thing that accelerates the collapse."

"Could be. Causality is a gorgeous knot. Loosen one end ..."

"It's worth considering, partner. We'll spread our empire faster. Then you can deal with the Aeternans."

He threw a nice curve.

"How did you know about ...?"

"I'm not an idiot. You've been steaming about those immortal pricks for centuries. Don't deny it, Royal. You have a plan."

I shrugged. "Could be." Hated to keep my partner at a distance, but I was sure Ixoca's so-called ears were burning. He also had a vital interest in that planet. His fellow Jewels settled deep within. "I suggest we save the debate for another time. Let's help Ixoca fulfill his goal then we'll finalize our own. Yes?"

"Sure, Royal. In the meantime, play it straight. No surprises."

I held up two fingers and smushed them together, a salute I picked up somewhere in my long journeys.

"On my honor, Moon."

"Still have some lying about?"

I smirked. "Nice. You do me proud."

We didn't end that day on the best of terms, but I refused to apologize. At times of discord, we circled around to a conciliatory reunion. Neither of us made mention of the topic for the next three days. We avoided it even after Bart detected *Symphony New World* yet again. The President really wanted us on the case. We focused instead on the drawdown of our civilians and the first departures of military to join our off-world operations.

By the penultimate day of evacuations, we whittled down close to the final seventy soldiers who would journey to Ixtapa plus the last ninety long-timers. Desperido was eerily quiet by its own meager standards. We shut down four modules, stripped them of essential equipment, and shuttled those items to other facilities.

Except for two dozen stubborn mole people who wanted to spend a final night in their own bed, the town had effectively shifted to Mods 1 through 8. Of the twenty who entered medpod in critical condition after the attack, five died, three recovered well enough to walk out on their own power, and eight left via Scramjet to rehabilitate on G'hladi. Four civilians remained, still hanging on but barely. If they showed no improvement before the final day, we'd have to make a difficult decision.

I thought of hosting a street party for the final Desperidans, none of whom intended to continue their lives with Black Star. However, our last party took a rather unfortunate turn. Neither Ship nor Elian seemed thrilled with the idea.

We settled on a nice dinner, with attendees spread out between

Mods 4 through 6. We ran our best recipes through kiosks and blended them with the superb greens from the hydrogardens. And, of course, we washed it down with the last of the cantina's inventory.

It went as well as any improvised affair comprised of people with nothing in common. Conversations were awkward, especially when they turned to future plans. The veterans seemed both jealous and disdainful of those who intended to retire in paradise, as many old-timers classified it. Though no vet made the accusation, I believe they saw these men and women as defectors at the dawn before battle.

As if these folks – most in their sixties and frequently drunk – offered anything of promise to Black Star. Elian assured us none contributed to Motif production, never displayed leadership qualities or a work ethic to be valued. They were derelicts who found their way into money through proximity. We'd uphold our promise to shuttle them to new lives elsewhere on Azteca or the system of their choice.

"Good riddance," Elian told us afterward. "If they stuck with us, we'd probably end up having to kill them, wipe their memories, or find a good desert to plant their asses in. Some people just ain't grateful."

Elian joined us gods on the dead-quiet western perimeter, where we enjoyed a last drink together under a starry sky.

"Fair point, my friend. Black Star requires an efficient work force. Don't need nibblers to gob up the machine, as they say."

Elian laughed. "Do they? Never heard that one before, Raul."

"Huh." I turned to Moon. "Is it something they say in Beta Universe? Maybe I heard it there."

He grunted. "Who knows, partner? You spent years causing trouble there long before we met."

Ouch.

"Whatever the case, it's all but done. Four flights tomorrow. Eleven destinations." I raised my flask. "Excellent work, Elian. Be proud."

110

"Thanks, Raul. Means a lot to me. Reckon I've learned a new skill."

"Which is?"

"I'm a decent travel agent. Most of the wafflers took my advice about where to settle."

Moon grabbed two cigars from his jacket, handing one to Elian.

"You gave them three options," Moon said. "One involved a tent in the southern Naugista, and the other overlooked a glacier on Inuit Kingdom. They chose the island with wide beaches and crystal green water. Shocking."

Elian smirked as he held the cigar between his lips, waiting for Moon's lighted finger.

"Hey, two gave serious thought to the glacier. It has a hell of a view. Cold as fuck, but a great view." He savored the first deep puffs and nodded to Moon's left hand. "I'm going to miss that little trick."

"Not for long."

Elian shrugged. "I know. It's only a few days. But like you both been saying: After we leave Azteca behind, we'll be traveling pretty regular. Lot of new worlds to break in. The deal-making alone ... it's a wild time. It just won't be like Desperido." He glanced over his shoulder at the dying town. "You two were never more than three minutes away. And after Ixoca, more like three seconds."

"Imagine," I mused. "We'll have to revert to manmade comms again. Almost primitive, but a fact of life. We can't rely on Ixoca's generosity forever."

I suspected Ixoca had other plans in that regard.

"I get you, Raul. At first, comm implants sound amazing. The Aeternans have been using a shared neural interface for something like twenty years. Always thought that was the way to go."

"And now?"

"Eh. It ain't right for mortals. Knowing someone could just pop in there at any second ..."

"And watch you take a piss," Moon said.

The banter stopped cold. Moon did not crack a smile or show the first hint of irony.

111

"Good one, Ilan." Elian thought about it. "You didn't actually ...?"

Moon pulled hard on his cigar, exhaled rings, and replied:

"No. But I enjoyed watching you masturbate."

I checked my laughter. In time, Elian came around to the joke.

"You had me going. I mean, you didn't actually?"

Moon scoffed. "I can be a sick sonofabitch, but not like that."

"Course not. I figured you were kidding around."

"I've known Ilan for centuries, my friend. He does not kid around. I'd go so far as to say he doesn't know how."

Moon took no offense. A master of witty repartee, he was not. Yet I gave him credit for trying.

My partner grunted his response.

"What Raul means to say is, I don't rehearse before I open my mouth. Unlike him."

No point in arguing.

"Life is a neverending performance, my friends. Those who do not rehearse for the next show receive poor notices."

Elian coughed on smoke as he laughed.

"I love watching you two play off each other. You couldn't be more different. How you stayed friends for so long ..."

Moon side-eyed me. "*Stayed* isn't accurate. We had our moments."

"Very true. The good thing, Elian, is we never had an option. When you're the only two of your kind from one end of the universe to the other, the bond cannot be severed. In our case, it's eternal."

The one-eyed drug lord smiled.

"To have someone like that in my life? Goddamn."

"You're fortunate, Elian. You have many people who depend on you. Love you, even."

His sigh said otherwise.

"Love the money I make for them. Yeah, sure. I got friends, but it's not the same. We're joined through Motif. That ain't what you'd call a permanent bond."

"It's a start. Still, I see your point. You would do well to cultivate an inner circle."

"Like a table of trust?"

"More than. At the table, we discuss business and strategy. You need friends who will stand beside you at the last." I didn't want to go too far into the weeds on this topic, but Elian needed to understand. "The same adulation you receive now will turn to jealousy and bitterness when your empire expands.

"One certainty: You will become a marked man. As your power grows, so will your isolation. If you're surrounded by a circle of people who adore Elian the money train, not the man, your paranoia will increase. You will look inward, and your fate will be sealed."

Smoke drifted from Elian's nostrils. I alluded to this topic early in his recovery; he had weeks to consider it.

"Guess I've never done well with friends. Not the true kind. I was a weird kid, and my classmates damn well knew it. Then I went psycho. That ain't a friend magnet. Truth is, the past eight months I came to think of you two as my best friends. Everyone else felt ordinary. Huh. I don't mix well with ordinary."

His words were likely meant more for Moon. They flirted with the notion of a genuine, lifelong bond – until Moon remembered he didn't mix well with humans.

"What about Leia?" I said. "She's not just your top designer. She admires your energy and perspicacity. Did you ever sleep with her?"

"Nah. A few close calls."

"Perfect. Keep it that way. Pay her a visit on G'hladi. See if you can spend a few hours together without talking business."

Oh, how lovely. I added 'therapist' to my many skills. Eh.

"You may be right, boss. I have a good verbal chemistry with Leia. Maybe I should give her a partnership stake. She could be my vice-president of operations. In fact, an interstellar empire needs a board of directors. I'll have to consider ..."

That went off the rails quickly. Just as well. I was a poor mentor in the matter of interpersonal relations, and Elian still struggled with his listening skills. Moon shook his head.

"You don't learn, Elian. You need to, in a hurry. My partner and I won't be there to catch you every time you fuck up."

Stern but fair words. I piggybacked.

"Ilan's right, my friend. When you leave in the morning, you may never set foot on this planet again. You won't be forever surrounded by Aztecan lackeys and sycophants. Your style won't sit well in every corner of the Collectorate. You'll have to adapt, become a chameleon. Assuming you succeed on both counts, you'll want to return home to people who care about the man, not the legend. Otherwise, all those shiny things you'll buy with your infinite wealth will amount to spit.

"My partner and I will walk the stars long after history forgets your name. We have the luxury of time. You, my friend, most certainly do not. Squander it at your peril."

On the positive, my remarks shut him up. Whether they'd serve him in the future remained an open question. To the negative: Elian deserved better. His strange genius brought us to the brink of our goal sooner than predicted.

We stayed outside for a bit longer but said little. I recalled the moment I met Elian, when he bounded out of the cantina to admire Bart and inquire about its specs. Such a harmless little bug, I thought at the time.

He proved me wrong. More or less.

When I suggested we retire for the night, Elian pulled on his cigar and tossed it into the red dust.

"Luckiest day of my life, meeting you two. And don't worry, Raul. History ain't gonna forget me."

Not for a few decades, perhaps. The most infamous humans tended to linger in the archival shadows longer than most. But what was a century or five? Barely a poke in Time's eye. Moon and I knew better than most.

When we returned to our bunker, Moon said:

"He'll be dead in a year."

"Ah. You settled for the optimistic prognosis."

Moon sighed. "At least he'll go out having fun."

"Humans. They never fail to surprise. Always ..."

114

I couldn't finish my sentence. Instead, my syneth mind drifted into a fogbank. I fell onto the bed and began to dream again.

13

I REMEMBERED THIS PLACE. A limestone cavern at the ocean's edge. What was it called? Ronin Swallows! Yes. I went here often when I was human. Young and full of revenge. I brought my victims here. Of course, they expected something very different. They fell for my promises and allowed me to lure them inside.

The man next to me had it coming.

I told him to watch his step. The limestone could be slippery. The tide was high, and the waves crashed inside the cavern. He was clueless. Nothing on this mind but a sexual meal.

We made our way around the perimeter to a flat surface I called the platform. I double-tapped a glow stick. Murky shadows. Water splashing against the platform's edge. Soon, I'd kill the bastard and toss him over. The tide would carry him out.

What was I then? Nineteen?

I undressed first. Yes. That was right. I wanted him to feel comfortable. He ran his hands across my chest. He asked about my tattoo. Yeah, I told him. I'm Green Sun.

Fifty-seven red rays emanating from a green sun directly above my heart. The pride of my youth. The group that taught me how to kill. For a flicker, I thought he wanted to know more.

Yeah, no. He used it as a precursor to run his hands up my chest, over my shoulders, and through my spectacular rainbow-colored braids. Damn. Those were the days. Best braids in Pinchon.

I allowed him to have a moment of pleasure, but there'd have to be limits. I'd say if he wanted more, all he had to do was strip and lie down on the hard rock. Nothing like the nasty bits on slick limestone.

He was ready. All he had to do was comply. I'd tell him my true purpose then shoot him in the chest.

So why didn't he comply?

No. This wasn't right.

The asshole removed his shirt, just as I remembered. But he stood there with blank eyes that stared through me.

Fine. If he wasn't going to follow instructions, I'd finish him now.

Yet I looked around, saw no clothes. Not mine or his. My pistol?

Something else changed, too. The waves no longer crashed against the cavern. Many shadows entered through the opening. They were huddled on a boat.

I asked who was there, but they weren't interested. Twelve leaped from the boat onto the rock platform. They surrounded my victim, all dressed in the same black cloak.

They whispered, but it was a jumbled mess. My victim seemed unafraid. Defeated eyes. Like nothing mattered, now or ever.

The twelve threw off their cloaks. I knew their faces.

My brothers and sisters of Green Sun. My fellow terrorists. Their chests emblazoned with the tattoo. This was the place where they died, where they were ambushed, where I exacted their revenge.

The tall one – I knew his name, it was on the tip of my tongue – pointed to me then to my victim's chest. He held out a foot-long serrated blade. The edges sparked.

The others subdued my victim and laid him flat on the rock. They stretched his limbs and held him taut. The tall one invited me forward to watch. He drove his knife into the victim's chest and carved.

Blood flowed as if from a lava field.

The man never closed his eyes. He showed no pain or fear.

When the tall one removed the blade, the chest was a red/orange quivering wasteland. I felt myself asking what it meant. Was there a message to be gleaned? Was this like the last time? More words to build upon the first dream?

The tall one laid a finger over his lips, telling me to shut up and pay attention.

I did. The bloody soup cleared, leaving behind specific carvings on the victim's chest.

Two symbols.

A hexagon with a straight line running through it from northeast to southwest and bisecting two small circles, each on the outside corner of the hexagon.

Beside it, an S tipped on its side. Similar to what I saw in the first dream, but with different symbols growing along the curvature. The claws of a yellow crab reached up from the bottom trough. A ladder descended from the upper curve.

After I studied them, fire sprouted from the symbols. The tall one backed away, and the others carried my victim onto the boat.

A wave of blue fire cooked the platform and turned it to ash.

I wanted to ask what in ten hells it meant. Why now?

It had to be *Father and Mother.*

Why?

Naturally, the dream ended without an answer.

I came to my senses after my syneth matrix restored balance. Moon hovered, glaring at me more curious than concerned.

"You're back, partner?"

I'd forgotten what a headache felt like. An immovable force pressed down upon my so-called skull.

"Interesting little journey, Moon. How long was I disoriented?"

"Seventeen minutes, give or take."

I pushed myself off the bed.

"You just stood there and stared? My entire matrix could've been undergoing a major glitch, and you simply ... observed?"

He tucked an unlit cigar between his teeth.

"Didn't want to interrupt the conversation."

"What conversation?"

"It was one-sided. At first, you were speaking to someone about intercourse on wet stone. By the end, you were asking what the symbols meant. I'd say you were having another dream."

I chuckled. "Brilliant deduction, my friend."

"Judging from the limited context, it sounds different from the first."

The details remained vivid; I'd yet to forget a single second of the first vision. I now believed these "dreams" were something else, perhaps messages on a timer embedded in my consciousness.

"Different yet the same, Moon. More knives carving symbols. And fire. A sterilizing swath of fire."

Did I dare delve into description? Would a second incident in eight days raise Ixoca's paranoia? I continued for the Jewel's benefit.

"Contrary to what our friend says, the merger is clearly having deleterious effects. It can't be denied, Moon. Not anymore. Sooner we complete our mission and decouple from Ixoca, the better. If we are experiencing a side effect, it might also impact Ixoca. I trust you're listening, my friend?"

The Jewel pixelated blue. She sighed with considerable distress.

"I do hope you're wrong, Royal. Once is an aberration. Twice is a concern. If it occurs again, please let me know at once."

"Ixoca, you delivered pieces of yourself into thousands of humans. Did none ever develop neurological problems as a result?"

She tapped a blue finger to her blue nose and paused for a beat.

"Not aware of any. Obviously, there were a few problem Children who lost their faith and had to be ... *managed*. You understand. Those glitches were not accidental."

Did she just confess to killing Children who went rogue? Interesting.

"Perhaps you'd look into the matter, Ixoca?"

"Happy to. I'll run diagnostics through my network heart. One cannot be too careful. Yes?"

"Of course, my friend. Thank you for taking this incident

seriously."

I waited until the Jewel vanished and grabbed my flask. The heavy pressure on my cerebral cortex dissipated.

"It's a time like this that I very much miss Theo." I raised my brow so Moon recognized my strategy. "He was an amazing interpreter of psychic phenomena. Wouldn't you agree?"

"He was outstanding. Almost on par with Addis."

Time to play our game.

"Amazing, isn't it, Moon? All the people we've met through the centuries, and none held a candle to Theo and Addis. When we were *maximos deos*, we could reach through time. It might have broken every law of the natural universe, but I surely wish we would've snapped them up and brought them along for the ride."

Moon did something unprecedented: He stuffed an unsmoked cigar back into his jacket.

"They were good listeners. The best. A damn sight better than these humans."

We went far enough. We could only call upon our *D'ru-shaya*s but so often before the Jewel became wise to our deception.

"Enough, already. We have a full day tomorrow. We say goodbye to Elian, the last of our civilians, and pare down the army to the final seventy. Whatever's glitching up here can't be allowed to interfere. The stakes are too high, my friend."

As with the first dream, I counted on Theo hearing my plea, recovering the data from this manufactured "dream," and assessing the symbology. I recognized none of it on my own. That troubled me. The core matrix should have been able to translate.

"I have an idea," Moon said, falling comfortably onto my bed. "We have several hours until sunrise. What do you say we change the subject? I'd like to restart the debate about Riyadh."

"Ugh. That again? We draw circles around the topic, never moving closer to the center. The timeline is clear. Benefit or no, saving the Prez is too dangerous."

He reserved his best grunt of the day for now.

"I don't disagree, partner. I'm not convinced, either. Do you want to leave a shred of doubt hanging in the air?"

I had none, but Moon's argument proved a welcome distraction. For the next six hours, we banged our so-called heads against the wall picking through the minutiae. When the sun rose, I found myself clinging to doubt. Goddamn Moon. Sometimes he could be an asshole of staggering proportion.

We tabled the matter and joined what remained of Desperido to begin a full morning of ceremonies and farewells. Shortly before midday, we joined Bett, a few sergeants, and Ship outside Bart.

"I still can't believe you're entrusting her to me," Elian said. "Feels like Bart should be here at the end."

"In a perfect world, my friend. She's not suitable for Ixtapa."

We intended to take Scramjet Maria and our newest acquisition, MX Transport Hidalgo, into the beast. Their size and specialized assets made more sense. Carlos Aylet, our ex-UNF quartermaster, oversaw the refits.

"Raul's full of shit," Moon said. "He insisted we take Bart, but smarter minds disagreed." He nodded toward Bett, who stood at stoic ease. "Bart's not a military vessel. It's better suited to your needs. It's our gift. Enjoy."

OK, so Moon was half right. I did push for Bart, knowing full well it wasn't the best choice. I fell into a trap called nostalgia. Eh. I never "insisted" and quickly conceded.

"It's my honor," Elian said, shaking everyone's hand. "She's a gorgeous creature. I'll take the best care."

"You're goddamn right," I said.

Elian laughed off my remark and acknowledged Bett.

"Commander, thank you for everything. We couldn't have done it without the men and women you recruited."

"True." She stepped forward and lowered her voice. "They're out there now, risking their lives to protect your business."

"*Our* business, Commander. We're all Black Star."

"Always fucking remember it, Elian. They might have forgotten what you did at Indonesia Prime and the lives it cost us. Not me. Put yourself ahead of my people again, and we will have a problem."

Couldn't say I blamed her. Elian offered no pithy retort or faux apology, but his body language begged for a quick exit. A tad more humble pie served him well.

"Understood, Commander."

He stepped through the egress to join Desperido's last eight civilians. He would drop them off at a loosely populated island on the southern continent of Bolivar before popping over to our facility at Ennoi for his first on-site inspection since the mess he made in the nearby Ularu jungle.

Elian took one last look at the place and grinned.

"You're right, Raul. The anus of Azteca. Who woulda thought?"

Minutes later, we watched Bart open an aperture south of the oasis dome. I expected to see my cerulean blue girl again soon, but nothing was certain. Too many wildcards had joined the game.

As we started toward the modules, I tried to break the ice with Bett. She had yet to soften since the 'traitor' affair.

"So, Stopper, did I hear correctly back there? You intend to stick around after we finish our business at Ixtapa."

She lit a cheroot and blew the smoke my way. Fortunately, a light breeze redirected it.

"Where you get that idea, Raul?"

"Your threat to Elian in the future tense. Certainly sounded like someone who doesn't have other plans."

"I told that psychotic fuck what he needed to hear. Don't read more into it."

"Fair enough."

She distanced herself from me and Moon; I doubted we'd have that conversation again. Too bad, really. I couldn't abide humans who held grudges. Always seemed like such a waste. I spent some of the best years of my youth murdering people to fulfill a grudge.

Yet we managed to maintain a professional relationship over the next three days. We devised alternate strategies depending upon what we found at Ixtapa, and trained the teams accordingly. We constructed a new comms interface to link in every soldier, though I quietly provided Ship with a special device, reserved solely for him and his gods. If I was right, Ixoca's many eyes would not be a factor at the most critical hour.

On the eleventh day after Ixoca extended his invitation, we gathered on central avenue for the last time. Bett ordered her soldiers to attention. Together, we watched the final supply ship leave Desperido.

Sgt. Manuel Kato soon reported in, along with his explosives team. He held out his tablet.

"We're set," he announced. "The detonators are active."

He handed the tablet to Bett, who inspected the layout. She transferred it to Moon.

"The honor is yours – just wait until we're in the air, please."

She snubbed me at the eleventh hour! Eh. I'd get over it.

Moon didn't appreciate her condescension. He grunted his thanks.

"Good work, Sergeant," I told Kato. "It should be quite the show."

Bett ordered Kato and his team to take their place at the front of the troops. He stood next to Ship, who Bett grudgingly promoted to Sergeant. It was either that, or I relieved her of command.

Far as I was concerned, Ship earned the promotion. During wartime, green soldiers rose in the ranks quickly to fill sudden voids. The young man was proud to wear our new (and fitting) all-black uniform, the weapons, the body armor, the helmet. He blended in with Bett's recruits, but he belonged to me. Ship knew what had to be done.

"It seems we're ready," I told Bett. "You first."

When we discussed departure protocol, I agreed to give her final word, but I went a different direction and conveniently forgot to notify Bett. She brushed off the slight and addressed her fighters:

"I brought you here on the promise of seeing justice done to the men and women who dishonored your service to this planet. Today, we take our biggest step toward that goal. I can't guarantee the conditions will match our intel, so be prepared for anything.

"These people you will be assigned to protect – the Children of Orpheus – stand for everything we do not. They're fanatics. They're a cult. You will have every reason to detest them. Resist the temptation. They believe we come as their allies to see their work finished safely. We will do nothing to draw their suspicion until they show their hand to Azteca. Then we deliver justice. And only then. Do I make myself perfectly fucking clear?"

As one, they shouted, "Yes, Commander!"

Bett wet her lips and turned to me.

"All yours. Keep the propaganda to a minimum."

Her advice felt hypocritical, but Bett was rapidly devolving from the coit I'd come to admire. Naturally, I ignored the request.

"Today, my friends, you are participants in living history. In my experience, damn few humans stand at the front line of great change. They live and die in relative anonymity. But you? The best of Black Star? The first to wear a uniform that will become legendary throughout the sector?

"You will change lives on Azteca and far beyond. There are many groups like the Children of Orpheus that wish to undo the peace and order created after the Swarm war. Once you eliminate these malgados, your work will continue beyond this star system.

"Black Star is not beholden to the limitations of the Collectorate Constitution or the UNF. We will expand our empire from system to system, infiltrating society through our choice commodities (my newest euphemism for 'Motif epidemic'). Through our long reach, we will eradicate other pockets of fanatics and anarchists.

"You will carry out the necessary work for which the Collectorate lacks a spine. In the end, Black Star will be hailed as saviors of the great interstellar union."

Naturally, that part was bullshit. Was I to tell them the truth about the atrocities they'd commit against their fellow humans? How 'fanatics and anarchists' were actually minor revolutionaries, law enforcement entities, cartels, and politicians?

Yeah, no.

I intended to inspire. Who wanted to think of himself as a murderous villain bent on the collapse of civilization? (Other than Moon and I, of course.)

"Understandably, you have certain trepidation about life after Azteca. Leaving your home world is not easy. Knowing you might never be welcomed back is terrifying. Forging a new life out there will pose challenges. Yet each of you has spent at least one rotation off-world for Black Star, in addition to your service in the war. You are the leaders we will count on in the years to come.

"For those reasons, I make an offer. Each of you will earn one hundred thousand UCVs for a successful mission."

As predicted, our fighters broke into cheers while Bett glared. Only Moon knew about the offer. I resumed when my army settled.

"Your loyalty to Black Star will guarantee justified hero status. But I ask: Is there a reason why heroes cannot also be wealthy? The slights of the past will be replaced by comfort and influence. Give your life to Black Star, see the galaxy, and wreak havoc upon your enemies. What do you say, my friends?"

In unison, they shouted at higher volume than Bett generated:

"Yes, boss!"

Was there ever any doubt who led this operation? Stopper faced important choices in her immediate future. If she made the wrong one ... oh, well.

I whispered in her ear:

"They're all yours, Commander."

She avoided a less-than-witty retort and ordered our fighters to the last ships in Desperido. She boarded the Hidalgo. I entered the Nav circle on Maria and waited for our half of the teams to take their still-seats. Ship hopped onto the transport, which we felt was a better starting location for him.

"Watch her carefully," I ordered him last night. "If you suspect anything, tell me at once. I can see through her eyes, but she's clever."

Ship didn't know what precisely to look for, but that was beside the point. Proximity was more important if she planned to make a move against us.

Had I developed a touch of paranoia? Absolutely. And why not? I carried a manipulative, possibly insane Jewel of Eternity inside my syneth; relied on my long-silent *D'ru-shaya* to decipher clues likely sent from the most powerful being in the nine universes; and embarked on a mission that might require me to do something unprecedented after two thousand years of enthralling adventures.

Like I told our fighters: Living history, my friends.

The Maria and the Hidalgo left Desperido and headed east to oversee the end of an era. I linked the hovering ships and threw open a giant holo for all to bear witness.

From two hundred meters away, we saw what the oasis dome projected to outsiders: The crumbling remains of a poor town with stone structures fit for no one.

"Commander Ortiz, if you will," I said.

From her seat in the bow of the Hidalgo, Bett deactivated the town's defenses.

"Grid is down," she announced. "Oasis dome is down."

And there it was. The old, the new, and the soon to vanish.

Lumen was right.

"In a few months, Desperido will be an empty shell," she said on her way out of town. "A hole in the desert."

See you soon, Lumen.

I turned to Moon.

"Any last words?"

He shrugged. "Good riddance."

My partner cracked me up.

"Eloquence was never your strong suit, my friend." I pointed to the tablet. "The red flashing dot will conclude the proceedings."

Moon brought no drama to the moment. He tapped the screen.

Down below, fiery blooms cascaded from one end of town to the other. They consumed the handsome new modules and centuries-old stone bunkers. A beautiful symphony of chaos quickly enveloped the annihilated debris in a burnt-red smoke cloud that hung over the desert.

"There you are," I announced to both ships. "A new era begins. What dreams may come. Speaking of: The first one awaits our pleasure at Ixtapa."

14

OUR SHIPS EXITED WORM outside the valley, safely behind one of its three surrounding mountains. On the slender chance of an ambush, we took a cautious approach. Maria and Hidalgo surveyed the valley for energy signatures.

"It's empty," Bett said. "Even if they're using something similar to an oasis dome, our sensors ought to see internal configurations."

"You're not wrong, Stopper — *if* the dome were similar. I suspect Ixoca designed a better class of shield cloak for his precious Ark Carrier. We hid for months; his Children have been at this for decades."

I waited for Ixoca to confirm my theory. He said nothing, but I imagined him watching with considerable glee. After an awkward silence, Bett came back:

"The fuck you recommend we do, Raul?"

"As we discussed: Patience. They know we're here."

Moon grunted his dissatisfaction but voiced it inside my mind.

"He gave us a slimmed down version of his shield tech. Explains how he knew exactly where to jump that transport outside Desperido."

"Afraid so, my friend. He calculated how much debris would burn through both layers. Ixoca is nothing if not precise. He terraformed this planet, after all."

A new voice echoed beside me. The Jewel pixelated red.

"Thank you, Raul. I appreciate the compliment. Like you, I believe patience and precision go hand in glove. I followed that principle in designing a cloak for the O'Shuma Valley. Its unique topographical features proved much more challenging than a simple dome over a small desert town. To quote Moon: Yours was a slimmed down version. Just flawed enough to leave vulnerability."

"Nice, but I don't see O'Shuma Valley listed on any map."

"It wouldn't be. Maxwell O'Shuma was Captain of Orpheus. The Chancellors named the valley in his memory. After the Collectorate fell, Aztecans erased Chancellor references. I honor him because he was a man of courage. He stood firm on the bridge to the very end. You saw him. I took you there. Yes?"

Indeed. Moon and I watched the Orpheus fall to its death moments before we met the Jewel beneath Todos Santos.

"Ah. You knew we'd arrive here someday. You expected me to inquire about the name. Very smooth, Ixoca. What now? You're walking around in their minds, too."

The Jewel sprouted human eyes amid that red face. They curled along with his heavy smile.

"Expect contact in mere seconds."

I searched for the two generals in question and narrowed my filters to Horatio Vargas and Martin Jimenez. I saw through their eyes and promptly ran into an impenetrable fogbank.

Oh, Ixoca, you clever bastard.

I long suspected the Jewel allowed me to see only what he felt was safe. How often did he switch out his many eyes for illusions, like security feeds running on a loop? To be fair: I'd have engaged in similar assholery were our positions reversed.

A voice radiated on both ships' flight decks.

"Attention, Scramjet Maria and MX Transport Hidalgo. This is Orpheus Command. Welcome. We're terribly excited to meet you."

OK then. A familiar voice. I replied:

"Senor Vargas, is that you?"

"Yes, Raul. Capt. Vargas now. Great to hear your voice. It's been too long. Please be advised, we have dropped the cloak's defense field. You're free to enter. We're sending precise coordinates to your Navs. You'll see the starboard landing port soon after you pass through the cloak. Once inside, Orpheus will take control of your Nav and set you down. Again, welcome."

The data came through.

"Away we go, Stopper."

"Into what?"

"What's old is new again, my friend." I adjusted Maria's course and pivoted to Moon. "How about that? Once a humble vintner, now Captain of an Ark Carrier. I like a man who doesn't limit himself."

Our course took us northeast through a canyon and into a wide open valley of lush forests and whatever else Ixoca wanted the world to see. We passed through a bubble with a thick electromagnetic shield. In the mere blink of an eye, O'Shuma Valley transformed.

I saw no trees, only a vast shadow cast upon a brown, razed landscape. Hundreds of residential modules, cranes, drone loaders, factories, and stanchions thirty meters high spread out beneath easily the largest spaceship in the sector.

"I'll be goddamn if that ain't a sight. Whatcha think, partner?"

Moon shrugged his shoulders.

"It's not the first."

I chuckled. What a perfect line.

We'd seen many such titans in our journey through the continuum, and I even vaguely remembered them while growing up on Hokkaido before the Chancellory fell. Yet I never encountered one berthed on a planet. It felt much more impressive – even glorious – against this backdrop rather than a speck amid the vacuum of space.

The Chancellors who designed these creatures were remarkable bastards in every other respect. But the sheer audacity to build these temples of god wannabes? I admired the assholes.

Reactions varied from our soldiers. Gasps. Choice profanities. Jaws agape. They also recognized this beast from a time when a fleet of its like orbited Azteca. Chancellors lived the high life up there,

130

occasionally sending down their peacekeepers to forcefully silence conflict. Order, courtesy of the Unification Guard.

The scanners validated my theory: Specs matched the archival data about Orpheus. She was 1.7 kilometers long, three hundred meters wide. Small by Carrier standards.

"A white whale," I said, a strange memory popping into my so-called head. The rest I shared in silence. "Remember our journeys through the Quaternary Universe, my friend?"

Moon grumbled. "They weren't interesting."

"I gained most of my literary prowess there. I recall a story about a man searching for a white whale that was tangible yet felt mythical. In the end, it killed him. Ultimate lesson in the futility of revenge. Behold: Myth and reality converge."

Moon scoffed. "Who's looking for revenge this time? Who's the whale going to kill?"

"Great questions. I'm excited to find out."

True to Vargas's word, Orpheus Command took control of our ships. That's how it used to work. The transport center on each Ark Carrier operated like a military base, overseeing an armada of battle Scrams, troop transports, and capital ships, plus an endless array of commercial shuttles and liners.

"I hope you'll accept my apology," Ixoca said. "I couldn't allow you to see our work until today."

"It's an impressive feat, my friend. Trust issues?"

"Naturally. In my position ..."

"Yes. I would've done the same. How did they pull it off, Ixoca? They might have built Orpheus under cloak, but that's an industrial city at its base. It had to be supplied from elsewhere. Surely, years of activity in this region would've been noticed."

"My Children are resourceful and well-connected. They ensured secrecy. Horatio is eager to explain."

I remembered my brief but fascinating visit to Vargas Vineyards. The man enjoyed spewing exposition.

"Fine. I'll leave it to our gracious host."

Maria and Hidalgo entered the Carrier through a portal one hundred meters square and came to a gentle landing on a hangar deck large enough to house twenty Desperidos. The white, sterile landscape was barren but for a few sedans and overland chasers.

A quick survey showed no one outside to greet us. Huh.

"We going with Plan A?" Bett asked.

"No. Let's escalate. My scan shows less than fifty people onboard. These ships used to house twenty-five thousand. We can safely disembark, my friend."

After we jumped out onto the hangar deck, my partner – a god who regularly mocked the inefficiencies of human endeavor (a trait I taught him) – gazed at the white expanse and said:

"This game was always larger than us, partner."

"Oh, yes, my friend. All those years we fiddled time away in the Fort of Inarra ... and this bad boy was rising. Impressed?"

"Ask me again in two days."

Nice answer.

We spoke barely above a whisper, but our voices carried. The two teams aligned themselves behind us and Bett, who we joined. Despite her otherwise disagreeable attitude, Commander Ortiz presented a humbled half-smile.

"Fucking thing goes on forever."

"That notion, I suspect, played into the design. The boundless splendor of the Chancellors. Ever been on one before today?"

"I was a kid when they retreated. Never thought I'd see the likes."

She wasn't indignant; no, Bett was scared.

"Wonder how many Aztecans will feel the same way when it rises out of this valley?"

Bett betrayed her smile with a sneer.

"It won't go down the way these lunatics think."

"The People's Collectorate won't be pleased either. Isn't there a law banning the construction of these ships?"

Her double-take said she had no idea.

"Wait, what?"

"Oh, yes. That's the real reason they hid it under a cloak. I'd love to hear Horatio's explanation. Speaking of ..." I pointed the length of the deck, from whence came four gently humming industrial rifters, capable of hauling two metric tons of cargo and/or squads of workers. "I believe the entertainment has arrived."

I recognized two of the navigators. One dressed like a man prepared to stroll through his vineyards, accompanied by a boy in a shepherd's robe. The other suited up for a day at the office; I'm sure he wanted my head on the nearest platter.

Horatio Vargas leaped from his rifter bearing the smile and open arms of a true salesman, just as Saul and I met him at the hacienda. Martin Jimenez did not budge, although his eyes possessed a killer instinct. I'm sure he holstered a pistol or two beneath that beautifully tailored blue suit. What he would've given for them at Conquillos Base.

"Welcome, welcome," Horatio said, shaking Bett's hands first. "Commander, I've heard a great deal. You've come so far from your misfortune after the road train incident."

Aside from raising a brow, Bett said nothing.

"Capt. Vargas, my friend," I said as we shook. "You opened the door that led us here."

"It was my privilege. And please. Horatio. My new rank is a long story; I won't bore you. Raul, I was so desperately sorry to hear about Saul. He struck me as a good man."

OK, so Ixoca worked hard to keep everyone here updated on our headlines.

"The best. May I introduce you to my partner, Ilan."

Moon drew Horatio's biggest smile, although Moon failed to respond with the same vigor. His stoicism did not faze the Captain.

"You, I have been waiting to meet. I was disappointed when you weren't able to join us at the vineyard."

Moon offered a weak handshake.

"Hmm. Sorry about that. I was needed elsewhere."

"Not to worry." Horatio turned his admiration to our troops. "Wow.

We were told you had new uniforms, but these are so ... what's the word? Ah, yes. Intimidating. In the best way, you see. Our people expect protection. They'll feel safe in your company."

The man was lying or being lied to. Maybe both. Fascinating.

"When do your people arrive?" Bett asked.

"The first sedans should appear in about six hours. Others will peter in through the night. We'll be at full capacity by midday tomorrow."

"We'll discuss security arrangements before then?"

Horatio rubbed her arm like an old friend. Bett bristled, but at least she didn't haul off and slap him.

"After the tour, we'll assign your soldiers to housing and commence with the agenda."

"Tour?"

"Oh, yes. Bow to stern. Full transparency. Orpheus takes some getting used to."

Interesting how he ignored the elephant on another rifter.

"We'd love to say hello to Senor Jimenez, my friend."

"Oh. Ah. Yes." His smile felt a bit less generous, but what choice did he have? Horatio pivoted. "Martin, please join us."

The former Governor of Monteria Province approached like a man encumbered by a straitjacket. He did not extend a hand. Then again, we murdered three of his most important allies. Longtime friends, I would assume. Hard to rally from that.

I went first. Seemed like the gentlemanly thing to do.

"Good to see you back on your feet again, Senor Jimenez."

Martin tucked his hands behind his back and sighed.

"I'm here out of obligation. Ixoca has made clear his plans: Black Star holds an important role in the future security of Azteca." He ignored Moon, having never met my partner. "I voiced my objection to your presence in this sacred place, but I was overruled. I'll perform any necessary task to assist your army, but know this: Justice *will be had*. I will be there when the sentence is carried out."

What a lovely greeting. Horatio cleared his throat and changed the subject in a damn hurry.

"Good. Excellent. Let's move on. Martin, you have duties elsewhere. I think. Yes?"

"Any duty is better than this. *Captain.*"

Not a happy fella. Martin turned on his heels with military polish and marched past his rifter toward a transport tube. Yeah, he was going to be trouble.

Horatio motioned for the boy to join us. Hmm. I recognized those saucer-shaped eyes.

"Everyone, this is my son, Paulo. Raul, you met him in ..."

I extended my hand, hoping he'd take it this time. He complied.

"Todos Santos. You did a fine job that day. Saul and I were impressed by your firm but reasonable touch."

The boy swallowed hard.

"Thank you, Senor. You were very agreeable."

"I'm glad to know you're still with us. The later incident claimed many of your fellow guardians. I wondered about you."

Paulo gave his father a side eye.

"I was shot on the rampart." He pointed to his right shoulder. "I recovered, all thanks to Ixoca."

"Good for him." I nodded toward Moon. "Odds are, my partner shot you. But we *were* in a defensive posture and also developed a nice relationship with Ixoca. I hope we can put the past behind."

He nodded. "Yes, Senor. We can."

I doubted Paulo meant those words – we killed many of his friends that night – but he likely had no choice in the matter.

"Magnificent," Horatio said. "Let's tour Orpheus! Paulo will Nav the second rifter. We can easily handle your entire detachment across the four."

We were soon on our way, eyes agog and jaws agape.

"Pay close attention," I said, popping into Ship's mind. "Get your bearings. When the time comes, you'll likely have to move quickly, and a rifter might not be at your immediate disposal."

"On it, boss."

When we exited the hangar deck, the rifters took us down into the heart of Orpheus, where a small city once operated. The stunning emptiness struck me. The habitation sector used to be legendary. Pastel-colored housing units for thousands. Wide, green parks. Waterfalls. Great golden statues. Transport rings. A levitating artificial sun beneath flying buttresses that separated the military and civilian worlds. At the far end, shielded from view, the great engine array, which powered these monsters across the stars.

Now, a hollowed-out canyon extended almost a mile to the engine hold. Several dozen housing units, each as dull as the modules of Desperido, clustered four tiers down along the port side.

"The Center Grand Concourse," Horatio announced, arms far apart. "Incomplete, as you can see."

"Am I to assume tomorrow's big event is happening a bit ahead of schedule?"

"Or long past due, depending on your perspective. Ixoca planned this for a thousand years. If not for the Chancellory, it would've happened long ago. Fortunately, the accoutrements are not important. They'll come in time. The fulfillment of the dream is all that matters."

"Ixoca said the Carrier is space-worthy."

Horatio pointed toward the stern.

"Most certainly. We ran the final engine and stress tests five days ago. She'll fly and she'll reach orbit."

"Your engine array ... what's the design?"

"Original specs and fuel system, Raul. We needed ion scoops for the traditional system engines in order to reach escape velocity. Carbedyne won't work on a vessel of this size. Ironically, our maiden voyage will be easier because we've barely begun the interior. Much less weight to drag through the atmosphere."

"Of course, if you had simply built the thing in space ..."

He tugged at his collar. A nervous tic, perhaps.

"I knew you'd bring it up. Best to deal with it now." He faced all our people. "Construction began twenty-nine years ago, not long after the Chancellory fell. Our ancestors spent centuries buying and hiding materials. The cloak over this valley allowed us to work unnoticed and yes, in violation of a People's Collectorate law.

"Our laborers were sworn to secrecy and paid well. Most have lived in the city beneath Orpheus since the early days. In recent years, many of their children joined the workforce. They knew the project violated interstellar law, but they persisted.

"Why? Because they were building something to last forever. A testament to our Aztecan history and culture, and to our origins on Earth. This ship will become the ultimate museum. A tribute to sacrifice, upheaval, and triumph. It will become a crucial destination for all Aztecans, but also a symbol of our unique destiny."

Sounded almost inspiring, until he admitted what I knew: He was full of shit.

"At least, this is what the workers were told. They don't belong to the Children of Orpheus, but we believe Ixoca will look favorably upon them after the fulfillment of his dream. Except for a skeleton crew, their work is done for now. They'll evacuate before Orpheus breaks it moorings. The ship's true purpose will become obvious to all at the Fulfillment Ceremony.

"Your presence at this juncture means everything. Desperido was not the only outpost making history beneath a cloak."

I popped into Moon's mind.

"As you said, my friend, a much larger game is afoot. It appears those who are the best liars will prevail."

Naturally, I bet all my chips on us.

The tour continued, but I focused my mental energy on how to win a game like no one had ever played before. Not even a god.

15

THREE HOURS LATER, AFTER our teams were assigned temporary quarters and duty rotations, I joined Moon on a maintenance platform outside the engine hold. We stared across the great white canyon nearly a mile long. The "city" part of city-ship was so vacant and white as to distort distance. I adjusted my optical sensors to sharpen depth perception.

Moon retrieved his first cigar since our arrival. I wagged a finger.

"Horatio said smoking was forbidden on Orpheus."

"Heard." Moon flicked the end of his finger and lit the tobacco. "Don't care."

"You say that now. Easy to do when we're playing hooky."

He released a blue stream of smoke that vanished amid the great white.

"I'll admit, Moon. Their rationale is no less bizarre than anything else about this ship. I find it hard to believe the colonists of that era forbid smoking of any kind among their tribes."

My partner chuckled.

"Horatio called them pure of heart and mind. When humans don't like what they've become, they try to find themselves in the past."

A little burst of philosophy from my partner! I was impressed.

"True. It's an ages-old tradition: 'We were innocent before.' No.

They were assholes then, too, just not as technologically advanced."

Moon grunted. "That's what all this is really about? Their great destiny is to return to their roots."

"For the Children of Orpheus, no doubt."

"And they expect to convince Aztecans to join them on this crusade for whatever in ten hells they're owed?"

"*Think*, my friend. *Think they're owed*. These people and their ancestors have followed one voice for over a thousand years. I'm sure the message never wavered."

I waited to see if Moon might fill in the blank. Instead, he puffed in patient silence. OK, fine.

"Ixoca's message can be summed up in three words: 'You are special.'" I waited until Moon groaned. "Yes, my friend. That one. The worst three words a human can be told from birth. For these eight hundred and seventeen fools, it's literally in their blood."

Moon fidgeted with his cigar. He never possessed a consequential ideology or an interest in the psychology of humans, but I sensed a change after we stepped onboard Orpheus.

"They'll fail, Royal. Won't matter if they win the day or become martyrs. Their cause is dead on arrival."

"Why?"

His eyes ballooned with pride in seeing the big picture.

"Wrong time. Wrong place."

"Very good, my friend. These idiots make the mistake of believing they're like the original Chancellors."

"Because they built this ship?"

"No. Money, subterfuge, and a cloak helped that along. Three thousand years ago, the Chancellors were no bigger than the Children of Orpheus today. A few hundred smug, wealthy assholes, the first of which was infected by a Jewel of Eternity. Remember? We watched when it happened. They built armies and conquered Earth because the human race was untamed. You see?"

That warranted a long, contemplative puff.

"Now there's peace and order. Humans aren't limited to one

planet. The task is too big."

"Hence, it will fail."

"Then why go to all this trouble? Ixoca said some of his Children lost faith along the way. They knew it wouldn't work. These people here aren't stupid. They know they're up against long goddamn odds."

A third voice entered our conversation.

"So glad you asked."

Right on cue.

Ixoca walked along the platform in full human form. He wore a shepherd's robe like Horatio's son.

"Ah. Felipe Marzalos. I suspected we might see you again."

Felipe's hair seemed more salt-and-pepper than last time.

"Isn't Orpheus every bit as exciting as promised, Royal?"

"Big. White. I'm not sold on its space-worthiness."

The Jewel found a snug spot between my partner and me.

"Beside the point, Royal. Now to your question, Moon. Why go to the trouble? I would respond to your question with more questions. At what point should humans limit themselves? Why must the ceiling be peace and order? Might some suggest those concepts to be mere euphemisms for oppression and decay?"

Moon reached out his cigar hand toward the white expanse.

"How does this raise the ceiling? How is their message better than peace and order?"

Felipe tsked-tsked, as if Moon were a student in error. Damn rude.

"You and Royal are agents of chaos. Yet you speak of peace and order as if they might prove acceptable alternatives."

"Not what I said."

Felipe backed away from the railing.

"But I know what you meant, Moon. You are critical of my ... of their approach to a new destiny."

Nice little slip, my friend.

Moon cooled his syneth with a drawn-out puff.

"I'm a god. I slaughtered millions just like them. Better even.

Royal and I lived outside time with one of the oldest races. They built a city-ship, too, except theirs was five light-years across. The Orpheus wouldn't qualify as one of their water rooms."

Feisty but fair. I loved it. The Jewel's frown suggested a different take, so I intervened.

"Felipe, if I may. My partner is merely expressing the opinion that size should not be a measure of greatness, though humans have long obsessed over such matters. So, yes. By mortal standards, these Ark Carriers are remarkable achievements. But they came to symbolize the inevitable largess of mortals in search of godhood. An attempt, I should note, that ultimately failed."

He tried to counter, but the Jewel's mouth wasn't as fast as mine.

"As you may be aware, Felipe, I enjoy a lovely metaphor. When I stare across this canyon in all its white, sterile glory, I see an intellectual vacuum. I see humans devoid of new ideas. And those, my friend, are the worst type of humans." I chuckled. "The second worst are teenagers. But I digress. This miserable class of humans can't exist as they are. They can't be satisfied with the mere blessed joy of breathing, eating, and fucking.

"And they need the likes of you whispering in their dreams for a thousand years to convince them to break an imagined ceiling. Sorry if we've touched a nerve, my friend, but we've tried to be honest with you from the start."

Yeah, no. Not even close.

Ixoca knew how to express disappointment through pouting. Felipe crossed his arms against his chest and looked away.

"You're accusing me of being a failure."

"Not you."

He rubbed his eyes. Was the malgado crying?

"After all my hard work and patience. On the very day I allow you to see the fruits of my labor, and you insult me so."

Oh, well. Time to talk to a Jewel like a five-year-old. Eh.

"It's not your fault. Moon and I don't blame you at all." Oh, sure we did. "It's the humans. They can't help themselves. When they reach for more than they deserve, it all goes tits up. They descend.

"That's where Moon and I differ in our approach to these fools. The last time they stood on the brink of annihilation, we threw them a safety net. But it wasn't an act of generosity or nobility. We wanted to save them for later. To have fun breaking them down again. Utterly cynical and thoroughly nihilistic.

"You, on the other hand, thought they could ascend to a new greatness under your munificent guidance. You would provide the spark to create the foundation of a new and greater homo sapiens. I think, perhaps, you saw yourself as a modern version of the Jewel who infected the first Chancellor. Perhaps you are. Even better, I'd say. But it's not about you anymore, Ixoca. It's these humans."

Now, that was a mouthful. I might even have been a tad bit sorry for bursting the bastard's bubble, except I was sure Ixoca realized these truths long ago. He didn't need a pair of fallen gods to show him the light. His charade was well practiced.

His subsequent stubbornness did not surprise me.

"I can't give up on them," Felipe said like a despondent father. "I have to believe they will honor the moment."

"Ah. And which moment would that be? The one where they announce you to the world and proclaim a new day for Aztecans? Or the one where they happily martyr themselves in your name? Assuming that's still the plan."

Felipe stared through us. His empty features spoke to a hint of confusion but more about indecision. Yet another moment where Ixoca had to choose: What words will best distract them from the truth?

He decided to fool us with the soft tone of a humble man.

"I have not decided. You are correct on one point, Moon: They are not the right group at the right time. I see it now. I believe martyrdom may be their redemption. But the civil war that follows will be long and torturous. I can't speak to its success in elevating my people. If I call off Shad Abdelmani and allow my Children to live after the Fulfillment Ceremony, they may build a strong enough following to reshape Aztecan culture, but it too will take generations."

He played it positively Shakespearean. He ran a weary hand across his face and pretended to wipe away sweat. A long, labored sigh followed. *Ugh. This guy!*

"I am genuinely torn. After all these centuries and so many plans, here I am at the end ... torn."

Yeah, no. Frustration about his Children might have been genuine, but not his plan. I knew the malgado's endgame, the only strategy that made picture perfect sense. Yet I needed to play his strings just a nudge more to verify our worst-case scenario. I tossed a little truth into the fray.

"Moon and I suspected you felt this way two months ago. When you willingly sacrificed two generals, we knew you had misgivings about your Children."

Felipe shoved his hands into his pockets and nodded.

"Anton Cherry and Maris Sylva were such grave disappointments. They came from fine families but lost their way. Their ambition focused on the self rather than the larger cause. I thought if they died and Martin sacrificed his public status, he would be humbled. As you heard earlier, his bitterness remains. He intends to kill you both before you leave Orpheus."

No headline there!

"He told you this?"

"Yes."

"And your response?"

"I reaffirmed your importance to the Children."

"But didn't bother to remove him."

"You can take care of yourselves."

"Not the point, my friend. I trust you won't mind if we eliminate him instead?"

Felipe winced at the notion.

"I'll speak to him again. He remains popular among my Children."

"Your call. He can't hurt us."

"Won't make a difference," Moon said. "If he doesn't go after *us*, an asshole like that will find another target. This is how they operate, Ixoca. Even if these people succeed, they'll turn on each other before long. Give it time; they'll betray you, too."

Felipe narrowed his eyes on my partner.

"What are you saying, Moon?"

"Stick to the plan. These people are deadweight. Better you be free of them. Black Star leaves Orpheus before Abdelmani destroys it. Then you can kick back, relax, and enjoy the show. See what humans are really like. My partner and I decouple from you and go on about our business. We'll unravel the rest of civilization."

So well said. Moon knew how to play this game. Now, for Ixoca to snip at the bait.

"You make a sound case," Felipe said, first with a sigh then with a sly little grin. "What fun you two will have out there. Chaos will not feel the same on every world. Will it?"

"Good question," I said. "We're eager to discover. It's been a long wait, my friend. But I'm sure whatever you have planned here will be its own special kind of madness."

"Yes, Royal. Still, I will be sad to see you go. We've been good together. Don't you think?"

"A marriage of convenience."

Oh, those pensive eyes betrayed everything.

"Indeed. I should go now, friends. My Children will arrive soon, and you have important tasks."

As he started to fade, I pointed to the platform near his feet.

"Felipe, one question. You have a shadow. How is that possible?"

I saw it the moment he appeared. The Jewel grimaced like a fella who'd been caught red-handed in the cookie jar.

"I ... I've been practicing since I first appeared before Bett. It's nothing more than a refinement of the program."

"Ah. But your shadow mimics your body's movements. It seems too precise. Can you assume solid form?"

"No. Not as such. It has to do with proximity to my heart. One of my terraform shafts lies directly beneath Orpheus. The closer I am to

144

my heart, the more detailed my projection."

Nice. Only in my wildest theories did I hit upon that one.

"You're not projecting from either of us, are you?"

Felipe pretended to shush me. What a lovely development.

"Oh, you clever boy. I'll bet you can shapeshift like us."

He nodded. "It requires a great deal of energy. Already, I'm exhausted. I should leave you to your work. We'll talk again."

Ixoca vanished, but not without having given away his truth.

Moon stared at the spot where he left us and then at me. He tapped his fingers against the balustrade. They formed a pleasant rhythm – enough to confirm he understood what lay in front of us. I matched his beat.

This endgame became a likely prospect from the moment we committed to the merge. We planned for its eventuality, but I had hoped Ixoca would be reasonable at the end. Simply uphold the deal and lord over the planet he terraformed.

Yeah, no.

He spent too long leading his Children to their destiny, only to be disappointed over and over. So few left – barely more than eight hundred. Certain to fail.

He was tired of them. More to the point, he was tired of Azteca. Time to move on. Time to wreak havoc throughout the sector.

Only one way to do that.

Bastard had no intention of leaving us. Hell, he intended to become us. As for Azteca?

Well, the Jewel gave the planet a makeover once before. Why not have another go at it?

16

THE FIRST SEDANS WERE EN ROUTE. I took advantage of our last chance to engulf Horatio's attention. We gathered on the multi-tiered command bridge along with Bett.

Two engineers, part of the skeleton crew soon to evacuate Orpheus, studied monitors from their stations at the forward-most tier. Beyond them, a theatrical viewport showed us the industrial city down below and one of three mountains guarding the valley.

This planet faced an apocalypse, the thought of which nagged at me. Yet I needed to compartmentalize. One concern at a time, thank you. Our plan would not succeed without answers to practical worries. I started with the white whale itself.

"Horatio, what's your flight experience? I found nothing in your official biography."

He scratched the nape of his neck, and his cheeks turned cherry.

"Minimal, I'm afraid. As I said earlier, how I came by my rank is a long story."

"Shorten it, please."

"Very well. I'm a figurehead. I'm neither controversial nor political. Ixoca felt such a face was needed when we deliver our message to the people. After Orpheus and Ixoca have gone public, we'll be able to appoint a full crew — they won't need to be comprised of his Children."

146

Bett threw up her hands with a quizzical swirl.

"You intend to take this ship into orbit without a proper crew?"

Horatio showed no offense at her tone.

"We'll have qualified personnel to carry out the launch. All three will be arriving in a few hours."

She inserted three fingers in his face.

"Have you lost your mind? I served on warships a hundred times smaller, and the command bridge required at least a half dozen officers. Too many goddamn things can go wrong."

I pressed on before Horatio responded.

"Let's begin with simple physics, my friend. I fail to see how you're going to launch 1.7 kilometers of ship with system engines."

"Ah. Yes. Quite correct, Raul. You see, no Ark Carrier has ever been built on the ground. The ion scoops will create massive forward acceleration to achieve escape velocity, but we need to be clear of these mountains before enabling the scoops."

Bett snapped back.

"That shit's been bothering me from the get-go."

"It's simple, really. We made one significant modification to the Orpheus." He led us to a nearby monitor, which featured technical layouts. Horatio zoomed in on the ship's belly. "She has been fitted with seven hundred booster rockets. Each will produce five million kilograms of thrust."

Bett shook her head. She wasn't buying it, either.

"How long will their fuel last?"

"Eighteen minutes, which is five more than we need to clear the valley and enable the ion scoops."

Moon and I ran stress tests on our tiny vessels before entering worm apertures for the first time, but they were children's toys by comparison. I feared few things, but this madness did not sit right.

"I hate to sound pessimistic, my friend, but there's a good reason the Chancellors built their Carriers in space. Orpheus has been moored to those stanchions for years. When the rockets fire, you'll have seven hundred firebombs destroying everything in this valley, including those stanchions. There's no contingency for failure, is there? Either we reach orbit, or everyone on this ship dies."

I must have raised my voice in an ugly fashion. The engineers closest to the bow stopped their work and stared at us, pale-faced. Horatio motioned for them to return to their duties.

"Trust me, everyone. Our engineers have run a million scenarios. The design will work."

"The best sims are no substitute for actual tests," Bett said.

"In a perfect world, Commander. We don't have the luxury of tests. Please keep in mind two factors. First: Orpheus is much lighter than a typical Carrier. Most of it, as you have seen, is an empty shell. Energy, lighting, air and water, limited housing. Second: The calculations originated from the best possible source: Ixoca."

Bett closed her eyes. Of course they did.

"Ixoca designed this planet," Horatio continued. "There is no greater engineer in the Collectorate."

No, that didn't sound crazy in the least.

"Why launch at all?" Moon said, asking the most practical question. "Broadcast the Fulfillment Ceremony and drop the cloak."

"The message is not enough, Ilan. Our launch will be seen globally and beyond. The valley, as Raul said, will burn beneath us. Orpheus will rise like the phoenix of ancient Earth mythology. It will return to a place in the heavens. The third largest object in the night sky. It will send an undeniable message that Azteca seeks a new direction."

Horatio struck me as a perfectly rational, sophisticated man with an ebullient personality and dashing good looks. Huh. Further proof that a lifetime of brainwashing can ensnare the best and brightest.

Before this went off the rails, I thought it best to calm anxieties and ameliorate the Jewel's likely doubts about us.

"I have concerns, but Ixoca is satisfied the ship will launch. And you're correct — the Jewel is a remarkable engineer. His makers, a race called the J'Hai, designed him to be. He was there when the original Orpheus crashed and knows the physics better than any of us. Horatio, we'd feel more comfortable speaking with the flight crew after they arrive. Will that pose a problem?"

"Not at all."

"Lovely. At what point during the Fulfillment Ceremony will the launch take place?"

He reached for his neck again.

"I can't say with precision, Raul. Ixoca was very specific: That detail must not be known to anyone outside his Children."

"Why?"

"All I'm allowed to say is that launch is contingent on his arrival."

"Ixoca will make an appearance?"

"Yes. The first time we've ever seen his face."

I popped into Bett's mind before she made a mistake.

"Keep your mouth shut, please. You were the first human to have a look at their deity, even if he did take the form of an Aztecan. Not sure how Horatio will handle the news. Play along."

She didn't hesitate to reply.

"I'm gonna get my people off this fucking ship, is what I'll do."

I smiled and reached out my hand to Horatio.

"We understand, my friend. The moment should belong to your people. We're merely the hired help."

"Thank you, Raul. And please, if you have any questions, don't hesitate. The crew knows the Orpheus system end to end. They were stationed here until a week ago. We sent them home to wrap up personal affairs. They'll live on the ship for the next several months at least."

"Very well. If you'll pardon us, Horatio, I'd like to consult with Black Star leadership."

His puny smile said the opposite of, "Take all the time you need, my friends."

After he left us alone, I pointed out the remaining pairs of ears near the bow.

"Go ahead, Bett. Get it off your chest, but quietly."

She let it rip.

"Has everybody lost their goddamn mind to Ixoca? I agreed to bring my fighters here for justice and to get that damn *thing* out of my head. This ship will never reach orbit."

"Normally, I'd agree. Horatio's outsized confidence does not inspire. But we've seen Ixoca's handiwork. He equipped his Children with the tools to make this launch succeed. He has too much to lose. Ilan?"

He grunted, knowing full damn well I required a united front.

"They've been building this whale close to thirty years. Stockpiling equipment for generations before then. These people may be halfway around the bend, but they have a solid plan."

Bett choked on her laughter. She must've seen that coming.

"You malgados realize ... if the three of us die, Elian will run Black Star. Your work will turn to shit, and my veterans will die for nothing."

Not a terrible point, actually. I improvised on the spot.

"How about this, my friend? We'll place Maria and Hidalgo on Black Alert before the Fulfillment Ceremony. The ships will be prepped for emergency evacuation. We'll withdraw our teams from their designated duty stations before the ceremony begins. They'll quietly retreat to the landing port by rifters. If the worst occurs, we'll leave the Children of Orpheus to their ultimate destiny, so to speak."

She mulled my plan with a steeled jaw.

"Normally, we'd call that 'turning tail.' In this case, I'd say it's another road to justice. One condition, Raul: I give the order. Not you or Ilan."

"Acceptable, Ilan?" He nodded. "Lovely. I'll leave it to you, Stopper. You have six qualified Navs. Choose two. Speak to them in confidence. Anything else?"

She glanced to and fro in a conspiratorial vein.

"You think Ixoca will object? I'm sure he's listening."

"No. It won't interfere with his plans. Our part in this drama begins after we reach orbit."

"Don't be so sure, Raul. That planning meeting earlier? Martin Jimenez never took his eyes off you and me. Asshole will move against us. He has a plan."

I knew how Moon wanted to squash that particular threat; no sense putting ideas into Bett's frenzied mind.

"We knew our actions at Conquillos would have consequences. We must take care, my friend."

I decided against telling her the Jewel shut off my ability to see through his top generals' eyes.

"Ixoca promised Martin's full cooperation. Moving against us would defy Ixoca. I doubt Senor Jimenez will risk it; but I've seen men like him consumed by revenge. My suggestion: If you see him coming, walk the other way but flex your trigger hand."

Bett scoffed on her way out.

"Thanks for the fucking reassurance."

Moon double-checked on the engineers down below. They showed no interest in us.

"She's right, partner. Letting him live is a mistake."

"One I'm willing to accept, so long as we achieve our ultimate aim. At the moment, I'm concerned about Bett. I'm not sure we can control her anymore."

Moon laughed. "Did we ever?"

"Eh. She served a purpose. Might be time to move on from her."

He grunted approval.

"When and where?"

"The instant she tries to subvert the plan."

"She won't risk a move if we're nearby."

"Nope."

"Who then? Ship?"

"I've been popping in. He knows what has to be done."

"Sure he's ready?"

"Ship embraces what he's become. He belongs to us for life."

"Your call, partner. I stand with you."

"Never a doubt, my friend."

Actually, I was filled with an array of doubt. The human threats were insignificant. They'd take their potshots but miss their targets more often than not. Yet Moon and I would have only one chance to remove Ixoca. Our weapons of choice? Unknown until we heard from our *D'ru-shayas*. Did they interpret the symbols in my dreams? Did they remain confident in the dangerous plan Theo shared with me weeks ago on Everdeen?

The next time we called for our *D'ru-shayas*, we'd have to work at a staggering speed. Ixoca would sense the betrayal within seconds. If we did not blind him to our purpose, he'd claim us and never let go.

A marriage of convenience, my ass.

We knew when Ixoca would be most vulnerable and timed our strike to that moment, yet doubt lingered. Why not go after him now? Secure a quick defeat, slaughter his brainwashed patsies, and ask Sgt. Kato to rig Orpheus like he did Desperido.

A nice, tidy finish. What better result for a Trojan horse?

Horatio wasn't the only one who knew ancient Earth mythology.

I immersed myself in these doubts for the next few hours, walking the breadth of Orpheus. Occasionally, I passed by our troops and lent support. Mostly, I kept my distance.

The first wave of Children arrived in sedans, transports, and chasers. I observed from a distance while my people checked them in against the digiforms Horatio provided. Though Ixoca advised the Children to expect a "protective guard" to greet them, I can't imagine they felt welcomed by soldiers in black. Most donned white smocks.

A guileless flock coming before the head shepherd.

Eh. Cults.

Seen one, hate them all.

Moon took flight to the engine hold for another smoke far from anyone who might protest, while I strutted along the perimeter of the residential habitats. The first Children settled in. They had no idea who I was, unaware I used to see through their eyes.

Until today, when Ixoca excised them from my purview. I knew of one such cultist who Ixoca had never allowed me to see. For a time, I didn't realize she was absent. Perhaps I'd merely lost interest.

That changed when I heard her call out from behind.

"You fucking malgado," she said. "I should have known."

I turned with the grace of a gentleman and tipped my hat.

"Hello, Lumen. Have you missed me?"

She'd lost weight. Or perhaps the white smock deceived me. I preferred Lumen in her traditional florals. They lent a certain gravitas now missing. Alas, she never got around to trimming her unibrow. Overall, a diminished presentation.

Except for the sneer, of course.

"Why were you allowed in here?"

I followed the sneer with a dulcet reply.

"I'm a loyal partner."

"You're a killer and a thief."

I chuckled. "Only when I see opportunity."

Hands to her hips, Lumen looked around for help.

"I won't stand for this. The Children of Orpheus don't know you like I do."

"Their opinion means nothing. I'm here at Ixoca's invitation. My army will protect your people through their coming trials. He told his Children to expect us."

She only now made the connection.

"*No.* Those soldiers ... they belong to you?"

"Desperido grew by leaps and bounds in your absence, my friend. If only you had stayed to witness the evolution."

Lumen pointed a finger in my face, but not for the first time. I let her anger play itself out.

"Not this time, Raul. You've taken enough. You're not here to protect us."

I side-stepped her indignant finger and approached with arms open in reconciliation.

"Come now, Lumen. We should park the past and move forward."

"Not in this lifetime. I'll speak to Horatio. I'll tell everyone what you did in my town. You'll be gone by the morning."

Huh. Time to prevent a kerfuffle, so I altered my tactics.

"Ixoca tells me you reunited with your grandchildren. He said you

153

were bringing them and their mother. Yes?"

Should I have just come right out and told her how Vash died? I assumed my favorite strategy — threaten loved ones — would snuff her tirade. Yeah, no. Error in judgment.

"Don't try, Raul. They're not here. Their mother blamed the Children of Orpheus for Vash. She wants nothing to do with us."

"Or you?"

I always struggled to crack Lumen's leather façade. This time, I detected a slight tear.

"You don't know how to stop taking."

"On the contrary. I give at every opportunity. For years, you diverted profits from those poor Desperidans pursuant to this overblown monstrosity. I opened doors and bank accounts. Now they're living the dream on seven different planets."

She knew nothing of this development, so I showered her with a bounty of updates.

"Oh, yes. They found true paradise with Black Star. The oldest have retired to live out their days in luxury and sunshine. The youngest help me build an empire. Oh, and you'll be happy to know I haven't gotten Ship killed. Thanks to your revelation, he managed to slaughter everyone on Everdeen who betrayed him. He can take care of himself. He's like me now. You'll see him before the Fulfillment Ceremony."

Lumen cleared her throat.

"He ... Ship's here?"

"I'm not sure if he'll thank you for the truth or shoot you for hiding it all those years."

I'd have to pop in and warn him to keep his cool.

"Where's your partner, Raul? Stalking his prey?"

"At the moment, likely enjoying a fine cigar. But I'll pass along your compliments."

Since this encounter had nothing else going for it, I resumed my walk. If Lumen cared to follow behind with prodigious insults, who was I to stop her?

"I'm sure I have many security matters to attend, old friend, so I'll let you settle in."

"This isn't over, Raul. Everyone here will know what you and Ilan truly are."

I waved farewell.

"Yes. Killers. Thieves. Precisely the kind of people one wouldn't expect the great Ixoca to invite to such a sacred event. I wonder what your fellow Children will think about his judgment? I'd take extraordinary care with what you say."

If only she possessed a weapon. She'd never have a cleaner shot.

"Oh, and Lumen. For future consideration: Desperido is now a hole in the ground. An empty palette perfect for someone looking to start from scratch."

I suppose it wasn't the nicest way to cut off our reunion. In another context, Lumen would've made for a fine ally. I imagined she would excel at a negotiating table. Sure, her principles and obstinance would likely get her killed, but only after achieving a fair deal for our side.

Very sad.

Lumen should have given up on the faith and stayed home with her grandchildren. Now, she'd almost certainly die with the rest of these fools. But how was that my problem?

I owed Lumen nothing. Like most humans, she followed her heart – usually a recipe for disaster of some degree.

Later, I mentioned the brief encounter to Moon, who said he should've killed her on Roadway 9 the night she bolted town.

"Would've been a mercy."

I agreed. Instead, she'd likely face a horrifying if not dramatic end. Yet another smart human who lost her faculties. Typical.

That night, as the arrival of Children accelerated, I assessed all the potential outcomes, wondered if *Father and Mother* had a final dream in store for me, maneuvered Ship closer to Bett, interviewed the Orpheus flight crew, and heard not one word from Ixoca.

How excited he must have been. Moon and I knew what it felt like to fulfill a dream after a thousand years of preparation. How devastating would it be to fall one day short of eternity?

When morning came to Orpheus, we intended to find out.

17

DURING THE NIGHT, Ixoca's Children rolled out a large carpet of artificial turf in the Grand Central Concourse where the ship's design called for a park. Horatio deemed the turf "down payment on the future."

"We'll have something soft beneath our feet when we welcome Ixoca," he said during a final discussion of logistics. "Per request, his Children must remove their shoes."

How sweet. Did he also intend to baptize them? A last rite before sending most of Azteca's billion people straight to hell? God wannabes never understood how to balance reverence with subservience. Their megalomaniacal tendencies interfered.

A stage fronted the improvised green space. Behind it, a wall-size holo projected a view of Founders Memorial and the giant engine shell of the original Orpheus.

Volunteers ferried their fellow faithful from the habitat units across a quarter mile and up three tiers. The green space rapidly filled with all imaginable shades of white. Smocks for the women; pants plus collar-free shirts for the men.

Fitting. Ixoca deemed today 'white sunset,' a name which likely carried multiple meanings. This gathering at the forward end of the concourse dipped my rating of humanity another notch. The Children filled ninety percent of the green space and appeared to blend into the backdrop of the endless white canyon. Three comms drones hovered over the scene.

This was all that remained of Ixoca's thousand years of work? These people had the audacity to think they inherited the future.

Utterly. Goddamn. Arrogant.

As it so happened, I was an expert on the subject!

Moon and I watched the event unfold from the concourse viewing platform fifty meters above the stage. What a strange juxtaposition. If Ixoca were a true god, this was where he'd appear before the masses. I wasn't so naïve to believe he intended to remind Moon and I of what we once were and might be again.

Yeah, no.

Ixoca gave himself the best of both worlds: He'd see these tiny creatures through our eyes while also lording over them up close.

I counted the minutes until we shut off one of those avenues.

Or so I hoped.

"There she is." Moon pointed. "Lumen. Near the back corner."

I sharpened my optical sensors to zoom in on the crowd. She was so tiny. So ... uninteresting.

"The irony is laughable, my friend. She claimed we stole every important thing in her life. Granted, it *was* a considerable inventory."

Moon finished my analysis.

"Look at her now, Royal. She surrendered herself to Ixoca."

"When all else is lost, blend in with the herd. Humans find it reassuring. Not like you or me. When we were kids, we knew our paths weren't meant to be shared."

"Except with each other."

Huh. Was my partner becoming sentimental in his old age?

"Speaking of, I only see a smattering of youngsters. Most of these people have children. Wonder why they brought so few along?"

Moon grunted his answer.

"Didn't want to get them killed. I'd wager they're as concerned about the launch as we are."

"Possibly, but I don't detect fear, my friend. See the smiles? The laughter? The chatter? These idiots can't wait for what comes next."

I examined my pom and listened to the Black Star bead in my ear. Most of our people quietly retreated to safe positions at or near the hangar deck. Navigators initiated Maria's and Hidalgo's primary systems in case Bett called for emergency evacuation.

Bett and three Sergeants – including Ship – watched developments from the command bridge, where flight engineers prepped Orpheus for her big day. One engineer served as Chief Navigation Officer onboard a UNF warship during the Swarm fight. That discovery gave Bett pause; a war veteran inside the cult?

"You told me they were working against us," Bett railed at me soon after interviewing the former Lt. Major.

"Oh, Stopper. It's possible to serve more than one master. I apologize for not thoroughly vetting the backstory of every Child of Orpheus. At least we know the Chief is highly qualified."

"Snark aside, Raul, ain't the Chief that worries me."

"Understood. Gravity doesn't let go without a fight. Stick to the plan, Bett. Do not panic."

Ship knew what had to be done if Bett acted rashly.

My pom's scan detected two others in the forward section, huddled inside an executive office down two tiers plus a hundred meters from the platform. They weren't Black Star.

"Interesting. Everyone in white should've reported by now. Horatio said only five Children would miss the ceremony: The flight crew and two broadcast technicians, all stationed on the command bridge. I see them. But these others ... huh."

"I'll go roust those bastards," Moon chuckled.

"No, my friend. We can't be distracted. But I wonder ..."

Horatio paced the stage as the appointed time approached. Was he waiting for these last two? My paranoid instincts searched for one potential explanation.

The answer arrived in short order.

"Martin Jimenez. I don't see him."

I opened the digiform my soldiers used to verify all newcomers.

"His son arrived this morning. Mario Jimenez. The only family

Martin brought onboard." I crosschecked the thirty-year-old's profile against the crowd of eight hundred, my eyes probing for Mario. "Nope. Not there either. Thoughts, my friend?"

Moon shrugged.

"How in ten hells should I know? Maybe one's got cold feet about this white sheet madness, trying to talk sense into the other. Or maybe they're planning a sideshow."

Hmm. Reasonable thesis.

"Jimenez vowed to see justice done. He might use the ceremony as cover to come after us."

Moon nodded, as if he thought I stumbled upon a revelation.

"When we'd least expect it, Royal. Clever man."

I glanced over my shoulder. Yep. Snipers could hit us from several angles. If they thought we'd be caught unaware ...

"No. That's too clever by half. Jimenez is an asshole, but he's not the type to do it himself, let alone send his son to finish the dirty work. At any rate, Ixoca wouldn't stand for it."

Unless ...

Nah. The Jewel was certifiable, but he wouldn't dare take such a risk. Yet I couldn't rule it out. If Jimenez and son caught us blind and filled us full of laser bolts, we wouldn't have each other's syneth reserves to count on.

We'd be at Ixoca's mercy. Forever.

Well, shit. Maybe it *was* worth the risk. Ixoca had to know we'd never consent to take him along for the ride. Our injuries would end any discussion of decoupling.

"Those assholes aren't our concern," I said for Ixoca's sake. "Still, we might as well tie up loose ends. Why don't you go and roust those malgados, Moon? Ceremony is still a few minutes away."

"If they don't cooperate?"

"Kill them. Two less Children of Orpheus won't make a difference at this point."

Moon's eyes twinkled with the thought of a father-son slaughter; but just as quickly, a third voice intervened.

"Please don't concern yourselves with the Jimenez men," Ixoca said, pixelating red. "I'm in the process of talking them out of a poor choice. Moon's presence will destroy my efforts. They may yet be saved."

Right on cue. Again.

Sonofabitch planned to assassinate us!

A preemptive attack. *Of course.* He assumed we'd move against him. That sealed it: Either our scheme worked, or we were fucked.

Eh. Wouldn't be the first time.

"Of course, my friend," I told the Jewel. "They're your Children. Handle them as you see fit."

"Thank you, Royal."

When Ixoca vanished, Moon nodded. He recognized the truth.

Dare we take the chance? Soon as we activated our gameplan, we'd be defenseless – assuming Theo and Addis made it work.

I gave Ixoca credit: The malgado understood the inner workings of causality like a master. The Jewel planned months ahead when he asked me to spare Martin's life at Conquillos. He laid everything out to perfection and nourished an assassin who'd seek justice at the moment Ixoca needed him most.

Traps within traps. Lies within lies.

A brilliant game. Not quite at the level of a god, but damn close.

Now, to disrupt the game.

"I have an idea, Moon. It's last minute."

"Oh?"

"We shouldn't be the only Black Star reps watching the ceremony in person. If our army is meant to defend these people going forward, I believe our fighters should bear witness. Agree?"

"Huh. Stopper won't like it. How many?"

I studied my pom and pointed to the unit physically closest.

"There. That group outside the lift. They'll fly over by rifter. If Bett gives the evac order, they'll be less than a minute from the ships. Closer than her bridge crew. How can she object?"

He grinned, knowing full well she'd have no say.

I tapped the ear bead for a private link.

"Sgt. Kato, please respond."

"Here, boss."

"You have a rifter on standby?"

"Yes, boss."

"Ilan and I request your team's company. If history is to be made, I'd like more eyes upon it."

"Certainly, Raul. But the Commander's order is ..."

"Not affected. You'll be safe in our hands."

"On our way, boss."

Black Star was a quasi-military operation. Chain of command was as flexible as I deemed it. Bett would complain when she saw movement and tell Kato to belay the order. To which I'd respond with a subtle reminder of her personal stakes.

My prediction came to pass without further animus; neither Jimenez left the executive office. The fighters spread along the platform for prime viewing and did not guard the entrances. If I arranged them in defensive positions, Ixoca would know we were onto his scheme.

We remained vulnerable, but the Jimenez duo wouldn't survive the mission. Ixoca might yet order them to commit suicide.

Below us, Horatio called his people to attention.

"Welcome, everyone, to a day our ancestors only dreamed about. Each of us should feel honored to experience this sacred event. Ixoca would say we are both the end and the beginning of a long, remarkable story. Soon, we will share our story with Azteca.

"I haven't had the good fortune of meeting everyone yet, but we'll have time after Orpheus returns to space. I am Capt. Horatio Vargas, yet I'm merely a conduit for today's ceremony. We have only one true Captain."

He led them in polite applause that rose to a crescendo.

"To the particulars," he continued. "Each of you has reviewed the rules for broadcast and launch. In order to achieve maximum impact on our global audience, your enthusiasm is crucial, but only cheer at moments where Ixoca pauses for dramatic effect. His words must be heard loud and clear."

How about that? Good old fashioned stage management.

"Now, his first appearance will cause a great stir. None of us have seen his face. When he manifests to physical form, he will allow you a moment to cry out his name. Do so in unison. When he has heard enough, he will signify silence by raising his left hand like so."

Nope. Not a sheep in sight!

"Ixoca will signal our flight engineers when he wants the world to see our miracle launch into space. We will drop our cloak and stun the Aztecan people. Orpheus will rise from a storm of fire. The climb will be difficult, but show no fear. Stand your ground. Secure cams on the exterior as well as sighter-drones positioned along the flight path will document our nineteen-minute journey."

Pulling out all the stops. Impressive. If Orpheus did crash and burn, home viewers would see quite the spectacle.

Horatio tapped his ear and paused for a beat.

"The broadcast team says we are sixty seconds from taking control of the global stream. This will be a first. Once we command the stream, our broadcast will feed into Azteca's interstellar news wave. In a matter of hours, citizens of all forty worlds will know what's happened in this valley. We'll become the center of the People's Collectorate."

Loved the ambition, even if horribly misguided. And how the hell long did they expect to disrupt the entire planet's stream?

"Paulo, son. It's time."

The saucer-eyed boy joined his father on stage but bowed his head. The kid wanted to be anywhere else, if I had to guess. What fun did Daddy Vargas have in store?

The comms drones activated, their movements no doubt designed to capture crowd reactions. I wanted to see their faces upon realizing what Ixoca actually intended for their planet.

I stood at Moon's side and contemplated our next gambit. Timing, as in all concerns, was everything.

"It's been a long, fruitful journey, my friend. Did it meet your expectations?"

He laughed like the seventeen-year-old boy I rescued twenty centuries ago.

"By about a thousand goddamn light-years, partner."

"Good. I think we're about to embark on something new."

"I'm excited."

We joined hands.

"Here's to us, Moon! Another two thousand years of mischief."

"Only two?"

He made me chuckle.

"We'll reassess down the road."

My pom showed no movement in the executive office. Yet. I'd follow the scan as long as my so-called eyes worked. That time was diminishing. When did Ixoca plan to spring his malgados?

Horatio opened the Fulfillment Ceremony by speaking to a planet.

"Good day, Aztecans of every distinction and faith. My name is Horatio Vargas, and I bring change to our world. I speak to you from Ixtapa, where Azteca's first Ark Carrier, the Orpheus, crashed more than eleven hundred years ago. Today, thanks to the tireless work of the descendants of those survivors, Orpheus will rise from the ashes, signaling a new dawn for our people.

"We are called the Children of Orpheus. We come from all walks of Aztecan life. For centuries, our ancestors have guarded the truth about this planet and its origin. We have listened to the voice of the one who designed our world, who crafted it from poisoned soil and unbreathable atmosphere. Without him, we would not have a planet to call our own."

Had to admit: The humble vintner carried a huge bat and swung for the fences, as they used to say. He gave Aztecans a brief overview about Jewels of Eternity and their role in terraforming most Collectorate worlds.

"The truth about what made the Collectorate possible has been hidden for too long," he said. "Today, after thousands of centuries of evolution, the Jewel which redesigned Azteca into the planet we know and love will come before us, launch the new Orpheus, and tell you why Azteca must strike out in a new direction apart from the repressive yoke of the People's Collectorate."

Wow. He covered so much ground, including words of insurrection. Heads everywhere must have been spinning. Either that, or they assumed somebody was having a laugh at their expense. In their shoes, I would've assumed the latter.

"First, see proof of the miracle we accomplished." He tapped his ear and waited a beat. "Our cloak has been removed. Your eyes are not deceiving you. Yes, it is an Ark Carrier. An exact replica of the Orpheus. It is not a bringer of terror, as the current interstellar government might tell you. This is the creation of Aztecan patriots, not Chancellors. We have no Unification Guard to suppress and silence your voices. You bear witness to the greatest industrial achievement of our time."

Big words. Mighty claims. All while sitting on top of seven hundred firebombs. Nice.

I scratched Moon's so-called palm, and he reciprocated. We began our descent into our syneth cores. The deepest, darkest passages where our old friends hid in wait.

Timing. Precision. I used Horatio's next words as a guide.

He did not let me down.

"He is here, Azteca. The Jewel of Eternity born Q6, now known as Ixoca. My son Paulo and I are direct descendants of the first Orpheus survivor who Ixoca saved."

OK, so that was new. Certainly explained why the Jewel leaned so heavily on Senor Vargas.

I called upon my *D'ru-shaya*.

"Any second now, Theo. Take him at his weakest moment."

The grumpy reply brought joy to my so-called heart.

"Ready to roll, dumbass."

165

18

IXOCA WENT FOR A SPLASHY ENTRANCE. He pixelated in red, ten meters tall. "I am many eyes," he said in the booming, cliched style humans might expect of a so-called god. He shifted blue, accentuating the feminine curvatures. "I am all of you." He coalesced into the neutral form but silver. "I have always watched you and hoped."

Naturally, his disciples were impressed, or so their tears claimed. The fools could just as easily have been watching a cheap holographic projection. Ixoca played to the audience.

"Before your ancestors arrived long ago, I evolved from this ..." He opened his left hand to reveal the blue, geometric AI construct that traveled space with its brethren for a million years. He closed his fist around it and continued. "... into a version to represent all humanity. Then I met you and came to love you.

"As the first colonists lay dying of a terrestrial virus, I walked into the dreams of the survivors. I shielded them while I cleansed the atmosphere of a threat to all humans."

Oh, how nice. A blatant lie, right out of the gate. He'd likely call it a lie of omission. Well, what did the asshole have to lose? The witnesses were long dead.

"Now, behold the first of my true believers, who kept the faith and passed it down to his progeny."

He became Felipe Marzalos. At ten meters tall, he was a tad more intimidating than the fella who first showed up in Desperido Control.

Whatever else he said wasn't important. Moon and I had more pressing business; the most delicate maneuver we ever attempted – and we performed acts of considerable madness in nine universes.

"Take us," we told Theo and Addis. *"Blind him."*

I felt as if a lasso snared me and yanked my human consciousness into the infinite dark. *"A moment of bliss,"* Theo promised when we first discussed the plan on Everdeen. *"Can't take you down if you resist, old man. Surrender all of yourself, or I'll have to let go before I splinter you into a thousand little pieces."*

Not a pleasant image. More to the point: A terminal proposition.

I fell backward into a pit deeper than death's abyss and saw my lives in a flash.

The day I fell in love. The day I sought revenge.

The day I stumbled between universes. The day I became a general.

The day I found my partner. The day we were reborn outside time.

The day we ascended. The day we saved Alpha universe.

The day we walked into Desperido.

What a goddamn sweet ride!

We wanted thousands more years like it, but we could not move forward without surrendering ourselves to the dominion of an AI planted inside us before we ascended. The dominion from where Theo and Addis observed, assisted, complained, ridiculed, and indulged their endless psychoses. The last place in Creation we wanted to see.

We did not fall alone. Theo and Addis lassoed our third partner.

"Catch him at a weak moment," Theo explained on Everdeen, *"and we can wall him off for a time. He'll be blind to your words and deeds, but we can't kill him without killing you."*

"No worries, my friend. We'll have time to sort it. Either we convince him to leave, or we box him into a hole where he'll never

escape."

Theo insisted he and Addis concocted theories on how to forcibly expel Ixoca, but the solution eluded them.

"Can't do everything at once, Royal. Without you or me to manage the syneth core, it will become inert."

Huh. Interesting.

"Inert, as in ...?"

"Frozen, dumbass. The organic construct won't be able to access its own central matrix. It will become unmanufactured syneth."

"Will my body hold together?"

"For a while. But you'll be as inflexible as a stone sculpture."

"As vulnerable, too?"

"Not at first. The syneth form will be impregnable, but enough stress will break the molecular bonds. If you go through with this scheme, old man, do not leave yourself vulnerable to attack."

Which was, of course, precisely what we did.

Eh. Timing.

Though my fall felt like years, it couldn't have lasted more than a second or two. I flipped upright and landed my feet on a solid surface inside the deep dark.

"Welcome to our little corner of your universe," Theo announced.

"Nice. How about turning on the lights?"

"Cool your syneth, Royal. We'll show you a good time after everybody checks in."

"Still missing folks?"

Theo's groan echoed through the endless night.

"They're close. Addis is trying to wall off Moon's piece of Ixoca."

"She'd best work fast. He might be out there entertaining the masses and having the time of his life, but he'll know something's up. That cunt will not be a happy tenant."

When I sat on the dock of Ship's family home, Theo outlined how he and Addis could snag our human consciousness plus the pieces of Ixoca's heart and bring all six of us into a single construct. I thought he'd gone round the bend. When the Creators inserted our *D'ru-*

shayas, they made the division clear: Theo and Addis would never have direct access to what remained of our humanity. They were solely responsible for looking after our syneth core.

Little did Moon or I know, those two pricks had been scheming to cheat their way in for centuries. We inadvertently showed them how. The special comms bridge we devised months ago for use at the Vargas Vineyards forced Theo and Addis to act as a conduit between Moon and I while she inserted a piece of herself inside Bart's data systems. Unbeknownst to us, the arrangement opened a back door.

Theo confessed on Everdeen. His contrition was shallow.

"We're the last two of our kind, Royal. We deserve better than to be treated as attendants on call."

Nobody was ever satisfied with their lot in life, even *D'ru-shayas*.

Very sad.

"If you lead us out of this regrettable merger, my friend, I promise to reconsider your place in our lives."

My so-called heart ached every time I made a promise. The odds for fulfillment were so slender.

I waited in the deep dark until I heard rustling nearby.

"That you, partner?" Moon said.

"If it's not, you're in serious trouble."

I got him to laugh. Still a rarity and a joy.

"Remember the years we spent in the dark?"

"Different times. We had no choice in the matter. I remember the first day we saw light again. I vowed never to go back."

Theo intervened.

"The light's there now, if you two assholes will look for it."

"How?"

"All your human memories are intact. Focus on one vivid moment from your first life. Hear the sound of your heartbeat, feel sun on your skin, read the colors. Organize them into a cohesive whole."

OK fine. I went back to Hokkaido. I walked the streets of Pinchon, my first love at my side. We hunted our prey for Green Sun. They ran, so we followed fleet of foot. We caught them and allowed them to make peace with their fate.

Theo interrupted.

"Find one?"

We responded in lockstep.

"Gotcha, Theo."

"Next: Transfer your memory to the present. Bring it here, to the Orpheus. Even though your syneth construct is inert, you can see through it — just like your D'ru-shayas always have."

The second I unlocked the sensory data, my eyes opened. My body couldn't move, but I looked out over the platform and saw Ixoca delivering his message to Azteca. The pom remained open in my stone hand. The two Jimenez men had left the executive office, heading our way.

Not a positive development.

The ear bead continued to relay reports from the command bridge and the hangar deck.

"Can I speak to them, Theo?"

"No. You can accept sensory data, but you can't respond while your syneth is inert."

"Better than nothing, my friend. Moon, you good?"

"I am."

"What now, Theo?"

He told us to hold on for a moment. Conditions were almost perfect for first light.

My attention shifted to Ixoca. Boisterous, arms flailing, he spoke of the Aztecan people's great destiny that he alone would forge.

Yeah, no. When a megalomaniac says, "I alone," it's time to run.

"Now comes the first great moment of your revival," Felipe Marzalos said. "I have instructed the Chief Engineer to launch Orpheus. Behold the phoenix."

As one, the Children of Orpheus fell to their knees. More of the scripted stage management. Or perhaps they decided there was no point in trying to stand through the rough ride ahead.

The window for Bett to deliver an emergency evacuation order would soon close. I heard nothing in the ear bud and couldn't tell Ship to belay Bett's order before she gave it.

What felt more helpless? Alone in the dark or sighted but unable to be heard?

"We have walled off Ixoca," a weary female voice said.

"Good job, Addis," Moon replied.

"What's next, my friends?"

"Dawn," the *D'ru-shayas* answered.

And so it was.

A pink painted sky greeted us atop a flat gray plane that never altered between us and the distant horizon. Moon and I stood shoulder to shoulder wearing the same gear as the day we entered Desperido.

"Resembles our old training ground," Moon said.

"Without the special toys. Thank you, Theo and Addis. Care to join us, or do you plan to keep us in suspense?"

"We're right here, to either side of you," Theo replied then Addis continued. "Ixoca's heart is fighting us. He's strong. As soon as he makes contact with his network, he'll break free. We need to talk while there's time."

Addis did not sound like the emotional basket case of reputation.

"Fair point, my friends. Have you determined how to expel him?"

Their hesitation was answer enough.

"He can be defeated, but the method is complicated," she said. "We can remove his consciousness and his heart from your syneth, but you'll have to live with unrefined Jewel energy for the rest of your lives. Those tentacles have embedded themselves too far inside your core to be removed under any circumstance."

Theo sighed. "Addis made the breakthrough. I was embarrassed. Never thought she had the savvy to find it before me."

"You've always carried a misogynistic streak, Theo," she said. "You misjudged my emotional intellect as weakness."

"I did. Regrettably."

"Excuse me, my friends. This ain't the time to work out your relationship issues. Might we focus on the present?"

The rumble of an earthquake echoed across the gray plane, but the sound came from outside. Orpheus rose.

The Ark Carrier howled, banged, trembled, and screeched. External cams showed a wall of fire rolling across the valley. The great white whale lumbered to break its moorings.

The time for evacuation had all but lapsed.

The Black Star team I dispatched to the platform grabbed for the nearest supports. The Jimenez vengeance squad approached from the nearest corridor.

Down below, Felipe appeared to lose interest in the rise of the phoenix. He swung around and glared upward at the platform.

"Royal's right," Moon said. "We need to move this conversation along. That asshole is on to us."

We knew the initial part of the plan would not give us much time.

"My dreams. Were you able to interpret the symbology?"

"Yes." Theo sounded shaky. "At first, I assumed it was a variant on the Creators' language."

The symbols glowed fire orange beneath our feet. First, the S/reptile with three horizontal lines that extended inward from the upper curve and a pyramid growing from the base of the lower curve. Beside it, a hexagon with a straight line running northeast to southwest and bisecting two small circles. Finally, the S tipped on its side. The claws of a crab reached from the bottom trough. A ladder descended from the upper curve.

"What is it actually, Theo?"

"J'Hai."

Of course! The idiots who designed the Jewels of Eternity.

"Wait. I should've been able to recognize the symbols. Moon and I traveled across the continuum. We saw the J'Hai evolve."

"No, old man. You gained a superficial understanding of their tongue and moved on. They were a dead race; you couldn't interact with them."

Moon nodded. "It's true. I remember now. They bored us."

172

"OK. Yeah, so that was an oversight. If this isn't their native tongue, what is it?"

"A programming language."

Now the picture cleared.

"Ah. For the Jewels."

"Somewhat. Royal, it's a failsafe code. It orders the central Jewel matrix to shut down every line. The J'Hai developed it after the Jewels became self-aware and turned against their designers. By the time the J'Hai perfected the program and sent the order, the Jewel construct had transformed beyond their grasp."

Good news, if ever there was such a thing.

"Well, hallefuckinglujah, my friend. We're in business."

Moon did not share my joy. He bent to his knees and ran his hands across the symbols.

"Theo, how do you know about this language? You were designed millions of years after the J'Hai were slaughtered. Even the Creators wouldn't have this information."

"I didn't. Nor did Addis. But what we do know is the prime signature for raw syneth. Inside that code is the Origin Stamp, which can be found in every element created by the Great Fire."

I saw where our dalliance was headed.

"You found the Origin Stamp in my dreams."

"Royal, your dreams were programs embedded inside your syneth long ago. Their images tapped into your memories and acted out like the human subconscious."

"Good. Makes sense. Gods don't dream. I knew it wasn't real. It had to come from *Father and Mother*. Yes?"

Moon stepped into the conversation.

"Partner, you're not hearing him."

I was, but honestly, I didn't want to admit the truth. Not yet.

Theo continued. "Royal, the history and technology of the J'Hai was embedded deep inside the program. When I recognized the Origin Stamp, I used a simple algorithm to unlock the rest. Those so-called dreams were timed to go off at precise moments in the

173

continuum."

I knew the answer to my next question but asked anyway.

"How long ago was it planted in my syneth?"

"In Collectorate terms, twenty standard years."

"What about *my* dream?" Moon asked.

"The same, old man."

Moon cursed under his breath.

Ah, shit. I knew *Father and Mother* hated us. It envied how we ascended from mere humans to universe-hopping rivals. It wasn't satisfied with hurling our asses into the Aztecan desert.

"I hate being right, my friends. In this case, I truly *despise* being right. I knew It sent us to Azteca for a reason. I said so months ago, Moon. But for *this*? Do we chalk up the irony to godly humor?"

"Can't deny it any longer, dumbass," Theo said. "*Father and Mother* didn't send you here to bide your time and build an empire. It sent you here to save a billion people from annihilation."

Waves of laughter churned in my imaginary gut and surged upward like a bad case of stomach acid. My mocking joy echoed across the long, gray plane. Moon didn't help me create a rowdy chorus, but he smiled at this most outrageous of contradictions.

"We tried the hero business once," I said after calming down and wiping my fake tears. "It ain't for us."

Theo chose that instant to take physical form. He was a dashing fellow of fiftysomething with designer outdoor wear and two shiny holstered pistols. He tipped his white hat and bent down beside me.

"I'd reckon you're out of options, old man. It's hero time, or all four of us will spend eternity bound to Ixoca. Listen to the echoes of the outside world."

Orpheus rattled worse than before. It hadn't yet cleared the mountains but also hadn't surrendered to gravity. However, a new set of panicked voices arose on the ear bead.

"What's happening out there?" Bett said. "*What is that?* Raul, Ilan. The fuck are you? Answer me!"

Theo filled in the blanks.

"The terraform shaft beneath us has activated. The valley is falling into the world's largest sinkhole. The mountains will follow. Soon, Ixoca will activate all three thousand shafts. Azteca as we know it will not survive for long."

Great. The hour of the apocalypse.

A time for heroes.

I couldn't stop laughing.

19

TURNED OUT, I WASN'T ALONE. Someone else chuckled along with me. The Jewel appeared on the gray plane.

"I'm glad you find this moment hilarious, Royal. I want camaraderie, but you lack sincerity."

He altered his look from the white-clothed charlatan onstage. This version wore my duster, wide-brimmed black hat, and spit-polished boots highlighted by Moon's trench coat. He settled his hands over a pair of black laser pistols.

"You're not one to talk, my friend. You have no fashion sense of your own."

Ixoca scoffed. "Have you not heard about imitation?"

"Oh, sure. Apparently, we should be flattered. Sorry! All I see is a lack of originality, Ixoca."

Addis stumbled into our midst. She cut a handsome figure – thirtysomething, slender, with woven blonde hair and pearlescent eyes. She too dressed for a fighter's life. Addis appeared to have borrowed Bett's style. She spoke through a labored breath.

"Apologies. I lost control of him."

"You fought well," Ixoca said. "I must applaud everyone. You caught me off my game. I never knew Royal and Moon had companions in their syneth. As you discovered, sweet girl, I recovery quickly."

Theo sighed. "My grip is also slipping, Royal. He'll be free soon."

"Doesn't matter at this point, Theo. We covered the important bits. Time to rid ourselves of a business partner."

Ixoca wrapped his hands around the pistols, although I couldn't imagine what good they'd do in this virtual environment.

"Your subterfuge disappoints me, Royal. We achieved so much in mere months. I never hurt either one of you. Nor would I."

I stuffed away my anger at *Father and Mother* and focused on the immediate enemy.

"Not in the short term," I said. "You'd go along for the ride. See the stars, bear witness to our chaos. You'd wait for us to become complacent. We'd take you for granted. Maybe even call you friend. After a few years, you'd burrow down so deep, you'd control our syneth matrix and invade our consciousness. Then one day, we'd open our eyes and have no memory of Royal or Moon."

Ixoca waited a moment to absorb my words, transitioning from stunned disbelief that we foresaw his plan into a thin, wide smile congratulating us for anticipating his ultimate goal.

"It will take time. I estimate fifteen standard years. Now that I'll have to fight your companions, too, it's possible you'll experience twenty or thirty pain-free years before I assimilate you."

Moon at last let loose with a hearty snicker.

"Thirty years? We measure our lives in centuries."

"I am familiar with the concept, Moon. I had hoped to provide you with the benefit of a generous retirement period. A delightful sunset, like the ones you and Royal admired in Desperido."

Moon turned his back on Ixoca and faced our eager little team.

"It's time to shut him down for good."

"Agreed, my friend. If we're to fulfill *Father and Mother's* asinine assignment, our third wheel needs to go. Theo? Addis?"

Their blank stares toward each other did not cast positive vibes.

"What?"

"There's a complication," Theo said. "We never got around to it before he escaped."

Ixoca waved.

"I'm standing right here! I can hear you."

The Jewel pointed to the glowing symbols beneath our feet.

"Do you mind if I have a closer look? They must be important."

He didn't wait for rebuttal. Ixoca contorted his arms like a rower. The symbols flipped around and slid toward the Jewel. He gave them a quick look and responded in a patronizing tone:

"This? You intended to end me with *this*? The J'Hai's failed code?"

"The thought came to mind," I said.

"The J'Hai waited until we were too many and far away. Even if you infected me with that code, I am too many and far away."

Time for the silent approach.

"Theo?"

"I'm here, old man."

"Loop in Addis and Moon."

"Certainly, but I'll have to set Ixoca free."

"Do it. We need both those malgados in one place anyway."

"Done, Royal."

Ixoca's identical twin joined his ... brethren? They were pieces of a whole, which gave me an interesting idea. I felt all three friends scratching around inside my consciousness.

"He's right," I told them. *"This code is designed to hit them all at once. Well, they're part of a network. Pieces of his heart."*

"Correct," Addis said. *"From here, we can only use the code to kill him one piece at a time. And slowly, at that."*

"Which will take too goddamn long," Moon added.

"Theo, you said before there was a complication. Tell us."

I had an unsettling fear of what rested behind his frown.

"If the code is implanted at the base of the correct terraform shaft, it would spread like an infection when the full network activated."

"Logistics aside, how do we know the correct shaft?"

Addis addressed my concern.

"The Orpheus was built above it."

Why didn't I make the connection from the get-go?

"That's the key! He brought down the first Carrier using power generated from this valley. That's why it crashed so close by. He was able to consume that ship so quickly because he was drawing from his original heart — not his thousands of migrated pieces."

"Yes," Addis said in a somber tone. *"Ixoca in his original form, as created by the J'Hai, lives beneath this valley."*

Our internal dialogue lasted mere fractions of a second. We could still act. I glanced to the outside world and saw the Carrier's status on my pom. It neared the top of the tallest mountain. Even if we returned to our syneth, ran at top speed, and commandeered Maria, we'd never make it out fast enough.

"We have the tool to end him and we know where to deliver it. I propose we barter for time and return later to finish the job."

Moon glared at our curious new foe(s).

"How, partner?"

"We surrender. But in a way he'll appreciate. Follow my lead."

I stepped in front of my team and sauntered toward the Ixocas. They tugged at their pistols.

"I don't believe killing me is in your plan, my friends. Moon and I wish to make a proposal."

The Ixocas stared at each other in mock surprise.

"Very wise choice," they said in unison.

"Simple. Us in exchange for Azteca. We guarantee your continued merger, but you'll have to shut down the terraform shafts. There will be no apocalypse today or any other."

Their combined frowns said otherwise.

"Ooh, sorry, Royal. It's a fair offer, but we're not in a bargaining mood. We intended to remake this planet for a species worthy of it. So, if you don't mind terribly, we'll destroy the world *and* have our way with you and Moon. Yes?"

What in ten hells was it about these god wannabes? They tasted a morsel of ultimate power and decided to grab the entire buffet.

"I see, Ixoca. So, how much longer until the planet feels the effect of three thousand terraform shafts inducing chaos?"

"Our heart will transmit when Orpheus achieves full escape velocity. We can't have you two dying with the rabble."

Nice one. *Rabble.* Pretty certain I described many humans that way.

"Give me a moment to consult with my team, Ixoca."

Setbacks were rare in our business but not unheard of.

"That could have gone better, my friends. I think we should repel these two pieces of shit and clean up what we can of the mess."

Moon shook his head.

"No, Royal. Father and Mother sent us here to save these people. I hate it as much as you, but It could have killed us twenty years ago."

"What are you saying, Moon?"

"There's another way. Am I right, Addis?"

She touched his arm like prepping an old, dear friend for hard news. Then Addis shaded her eyes.

"Your dream," she told Moon. *"Theo and I studied it."*

"And?"

"Father and Mother embedded a message."

"I'm sorry," I intervened. *"What are we discussing?"*

Moon crossed his arms.

"Like most things, partner, you made today about yourself. I told you my dream. Remember? In my father's lab? I saw high-ranking Swarm officers huddled around a device that fired a laser at a target I couldn't see. They were staring into fire."

He was right. I'd forgotten about it, especially since there wasn't a second dream. No symbols. No ...

"Last night, Royal, I experienced a flash. I didn't tell you because I

couldn't describe it. Now that we know what the dreams were, I'm sure the flash was important. What was the message, Addis?'

She didn't want to say it. Somehow, I didn't want to hear it.

"It was the most complex syneth code I've ever digested. It instructs you on how to create a fusion bomb."

Yeah, no. We weren't going down that avenue.

"Insane, Addis. An object so complex would require more syneth than we can ..."

Moon finished my sentence: *"Live on."*

"Nope. Ain't going that route, my friends. This planet just might have to take one for the species."

Moon balled his fists into a hard shell. I'd seen this before – every time he tried to stand up against me. Old habits ...

"This will happen, Royal, because it already did. You know it's the truth."

"What I know is that causality is an endless knot of choices. Screw the continuum. It's not set in stone."

Moon gently pushed Addis away and bore down on me. Many a human saw those deranged eyes in the seconds before they took their last breath.

"Enough with the denial, partner. Father and Mother gave us a second chance, but there was always a price. We were just too goddamn naïve to see it."

"You're wrong, Moon. We will ..."

"Shut the fuck up, Royal, and listen." His sudden burst of passion came from a place I'd never seen. *"We studied the timeline before we fought Father and Mother. We saw exile on Azteca. We saw our opportunity with the President and the sudden rise of our empire of chaos. But we never understood how the empire came to be. Royal, we talked about this thousands of times over the years."*

I hated when he was right.

"What are you suggesting? Father and Mother blinded us to the truth? That It hid Ixoca, our army, and Desperido?"

"There have always been gaps, partner. How else could It have

known when to release our dreams? It set literal timers inside our syneth before It tossed us away. This has to happen."

Our *D'ru-shayas* did not object. Addis was unusually composed and Theo strangely subdued. Damned if I was about to fall in line.

"Tell me, Moon. If a syneth fusion bomb will destroy Ixoca, why send the shutdown code? Seems redundant, don't you think?"

Moon turned to Addis, who stepped forward.

"Because, Royal, we cannot reach Ixoca's heart in time if his pieces know what we intend. The nanosecond he learns of our plan, he will trigger the network. This planet will become like it was a billion years ago. Fire from below and a blanket of ash covering the sky."

Moon finished with the answer I predicted.

"You'll deliver the shutdown code to these two assholes. It won't kill them right away, but it will cripple them. They won't be able to communicate with Ixoca's heart. Addis and I will do the rest."

Ah, shit. I couldn't believe I was listening, or that every instinct said he was right.

"How will you deliver it, my friend?"

"Look outside. What do you see?"

Felipe remained on stage, hands held skyward, still preaching about a new day for Azteca. His moronic followers held on to each other as the turbulent ship reached the height it needed to activate system engines. I heard the Chief Flight Engineer announce the next stage.

"Ixoca's using all his energy to push us skyward," Addis said. *"It's not just the system engines and ion scoops. Part of this ship's power is being channeled from Ixoca's heart."*

The puzzle quickly cleared.

"The bastard has come full circle."

Moon nodded. *"He's expending all his energy to make sure we reach orbit. If we die, he'll never leave Azteca and walk the stars. We have to go now. He won't see us coming, Royal."*

Moon glared over my shoulder. I swung around to see dozens ...

no, hundreds ... of Ixocas spread out across the plane.

"I am too many and far away," one of the malgados said. Whether it was my piece of Ixoca or Moon's talking ... eh, who cared?

"They're not real, my friend. Just echoes."

"Perhaps, Royal. I wanted you to see how beautiful our partnership can become. My evolution and your cooperation will allow us to spread a message through this sector and beyond. Put away your foolish plans. Accept my embrace. Bear witness to an end and a beginning."

I'd been caught in many a sticky wicket but always managed to slip away. A happy ending for Royal!

Maybe not today.

"We're leaving," Moon said. *"There's no more time."*

"Dreadful idea, my friend. You know how it ends."

He shrugged. Very much a Moon response.

"Won't be so awful. Remember, Royal. I love fire."

"No. What you love is the slaughter. Fire is a mere by-product. You destroy worlds, my friend, not save them."

A mischievous smile broke through his beard.

"I believe that's the problem, Royal. It's why Father and Mother is sending me. Something about balancing the scales."

"Huh. A billion saved? Won't come close to a balance."

He slapped both hands on my so-called shoulders.

"Maybe you'll make up the difference someday, partner."

"Not a fucking chance, my friend."

Addis grabbed his arm and swung him around. They shared a glance with Theo.

"Translate the code," Addis told her fellow *D'ru-shaya*. *"He must deliver it as soon as we leave. Save the other for later."*

Theo bowed to her like she was a princess.

"I wish we had become better friends. I have countless regrets."

"The translation, Theo. Deliver it now."

The J'Hai's programming language took shape inside my consciousness. In an instant, I learned to speak it as well as

Engleshe. Moon and Addis nodded toward our enemy.

I faced the Ixocas.

"I fear we cannot accept your embrace, my friend. But we do have an official response to your proposal. Listen carefully."

Oh, how our fate might have been different if the J'Hai hadn't waited so long to deliver the shutdown code.

"En-iz'l ack*fac'n ka-xxus 6-qa. En-iz'l ack*fac'n ka-xxus 6-qa."

Theo told me not to let up, that even the slightest break might open the wrong door.

I never looked back because I knew he wouldn't be there.

Instead, I turned my eyes to the outside world. My body remained inert, but my partner's syneth came alive. He shook off the rust, stretched his legs, and assessed his situation.

Moon stared at my handsome statue and tipped his hat. Then he disappeared in a blur, racing toward the hangar deck at fifty times human speed.

The Ixocas enjoyed a hearty laugh as I repeated the code.

"Why, look! Royal thinks he's a J'Hai," said one.

"He must hate losing," another responded. "How long he has been around? Two thousand years?"

"Goodness. He's barely a child. Please, Royal. You're making a scene. And wherever did your partner go in such a hurry?"

I wanted to respond, but my lips were occupied. Theo stepped in.

"A child?" He said. "You two dumbasses got no idea what you're playing at. As for his partner, why ask Royal? Can't you see through Moon's eyes?"

Their arrogance took a hit. Wiped away those fucking smiles.

"Where ...?" Said one.

"Whatever you're attempting will not work," the other added. "We are too many and far away."

"Not at the moment, assholes. Try talking to your heart."

The hundreds of echoes vanished, leaving my piece of Ixoca alone beside Moon's. I sped up the delivery.

"En-iz'l ack*fac'n ka-xxus 6-qa. En-iz'l ack*fac'n ka-xxus 6-qa."

"We cannot be silenced."

They reached for their guns. Desperate times, desperate measures.

"Go ahead," Theo said. "Fire them."

They accepted the challenge but the pistols never left the holsters. They were stuck, much like their legs in a thick gray muck.

Now came the panic.

"I'd say this child of mine has done you wrong," Theo said, shifting to a lovely old-fashioned drawl.

"We ... too many ... and far away."

The Ixocas slurred their words.

"Don't let up, old man," Theo said. *"He hasn't cleared Orpheus."*

"No worries, my friend. I can still see through his eyes."

I incapacitated Ixoca, but I had not yet killed either piece – Moon's or mine. I watched my oldest friend race across the hangar deck, leap inside Maria, and order the chosen Nav to leave. He grabbed the controls and set coordinates on the worm drive.

Of course. A more direct route.

"What do you think of my plan?" Moon asked.

He knew I was there.

"You always wanted to go straight for the kill shot, my friend."

"Yeah, and you held me back almost every goddamn time."

"Piece of advice: Don't open the aperture until you clear Orpheus. It won't end well for anyone."

He chuckled.

"You never gave me enough credit for not being a dumbass."

Maria swung about and pressed toward the docking portal.

"On the contrary, my friend. I always thought of you as the most loyal, consistent, and dependable dumbass the universe ever knew. Mighty praise. Yes?"

He ignited Maria's Carbedyne nacelles and shot her through the portal several times faster than the recommended speed. She skipped along a cloud bank.

"Orpheus will be at escape velocity in seconds," Moon said. *"I have*

to go, Royal. Thank you for two thousand years. Can't have asked for better."

"It's been a damn fine journey, my friend."

At the final glimpse, I saw his limbs dissolve into pure syneth. He became something else. Just before he lost his sight and I felt him and his *D'ru-shaya* drift away, an aperture opened in front of Maria.

"Only a few more seconds," Theo said. *"Then it will be over."*

It already was for one Ixoca. My partner's piece of the Jewel's heart screamed and twisted then burned to a cinder.

The remaining piece shouted.

"What have you done, Royal?"

"Not enough."

When I stopped delivering the code, Ixoca had perhaps a second or two of understanding. But no more.

Long ago, I would've taken joy in his bloody screams. I would've watched with immense satisfaction as the ten-meter Felipe Marzalos phase-shifted on stage into red and blue pixelations and begged for mercy. At that moment, however, I didn't particularly give a shit one way or the other.

When my piece of the Jewel also disintegrated and Felipe vanished from the stage, I knew what happened in the place they used to call the O'Shuma Valley.

I licked my so-called lips and approached my *D'ru-shaya*.

"Theo?"

"Yes, Royal?"

"I'm not having a good day."

Theo shook his head.

"Nor me."

"I need to lift my spirits."

"How can I help?"

"Return me to my body. I have business to settle."

Theo grinned.

"With assholes?"

"Every goddamn one."

"Perfect, old man."

Yeah, no. This day wasn't done by a long shot.

20

I AWOKE TO THE HOWL of an Ark Carrier in more than a little distress. The g-forces had lessened and the turbulence created a steady vibration, but it too dimmed. We'd soon be in orbit if this monster kept itself whole.

My legs behaved like clay at first, but I moved well enough to analyze the situation in every direction. I checked my so-called body for laser burn marks and found none. The first positive.

The mess of corpses behind me revealed why I survived.

Three Black Star fighters lay dead, one at my feet. The culprits were a contorted, bloody mess after my men took care of them.

Martin Jimenez tried for justice. I gave him a gold star for effort but a giant F for bringing his son into it.

Eh. So much for their family legacy.

"Boss, what in ten hells happened?"

Sgt. Manuel Kato held his bloodied left arm tight against his body. He looked like a man who'd been tossed around in a cyclotron.

"Good work, Sergeant. You got them. Nasty malgados. Yes?"

The other fighters gathered themselves together, but they were still dazed.

"Raul, we don't understand what's going on. You and Ilan were ... I don't ... we thought you were dead. Then Ilan was alive and he ran off. We don't understand."

"Neither do I, my friend. Is the rifter nearby?"

187

"Yes, boss."

"Load the bodies of your men and take them to the hangar deck. We'll need to make room for everyone on the Hidalgo."

"What about the Maria?"

Nope. Not now.

"Follow my instructions. And Sgt. Kato, do not accept any order unless it comes from me. Understood?"

He was too confused to be counted on, but he wasn't important.

"Yes, boss. W-We're on it."

I returned to the viewing platform and examined the scene below. It was more pathetic than I might have predicted.

Eight hundred humans, guided (well, brainwashed) all their lives by a single voice in their dreams, were suddenly free. They might as well have been stranded naked in the desert. Their collective cries were almost as loud as the final shriek before Ixoca exited stage right.

I muttered, "In a moment, my friends," then tapped my ear bead.

"Command bridge, what's our status?"

Bett sounded like she'd heard from a ghost.

"What ... Raul. You're alive?"

"I have all ten fingers, and they're wiggling. Yes, I'm alive. Whatever you might've heard or hoped for appears to be premature."

"Ilan commandeered Maria and jumped to worm. What ..."

"I asked for a status update. Assuming the Chief Flight Engineer isn't dead, I'm sure the information is readily available."

I heard a contentious exchange between Bett and someone else. In the meantime, I linked in separately with Ship.

"Still with us, my friend?"

"Yes, boss. It's been rough going, but I'm here."

"Good. Listen carefully. Ixoca is dead. Tell no one."

"Wuh? Uh. Yes, boss."

"Stay close to her. She'll try to make a move against me. You know what to do."

The quiver in his voice disappeared. The kid stiffened.

188

"Gotcha, boss."

Bett returned to the link.

"Raul, the engineer says we're in low orbit. He's trying to push Orpheus to a stable position, but there are problems with the engine array. The ion scoops failed sooner than expected."

A better report than I would've predicted at this stage.

"I'm sure it will be the first of many failures."

"The fuck just happened, Raul? I can't hear the voice in my head anymore. Ixoca went insane on stage and vanished."

"Hmm. Sounds dramatic. Did the flight crew cut the broadcast?"

"Yes. But they're acting strange. The engineers are in a fog."

"Patience, my friend. They'll see clearly before the day is done. Stay at your post, Commander. I'll be there soon."

"Raul, if you ..."

I cut her off, of course. Much more pressing business to attend. I glanced over the edge and considered the fifty-meter drop.

"Theo, has my syneth regenerated well enough to handle it?"

"Yes, Royal, but you could also run. It won't take much longer."

"A one-word answer would have sufficed. The direct route is much more theatrical, my friend."

"Then go for it, old man."

I flung myself over the edge. I loved to fly, even if for a few seconds. Reminded me of the glory days. Star to star. Moon at my side. *Maximos deos.*

And now, these assholes.

I landed softly, although my feet felt a bit like rubber.

"Not perfect, Theo, but a solid rebound. Fine work, my friend."

"Compliment taken, Royal."

"We should discuss a new working arrangement. Agree?"

"Love to."

But first, to the rabble.

I unholstered my pistols and walked to the center of the stage where the image of long-dead Felipe Marzalos tried to con a billion people into a bright new future.

These people were as battered by the ascent as they were by their loss and grief. Several exited their daze when I arrived. More quickly followed. Did they wonder if there was hope, after all? Did they think I might be Ixoca reborn?

Eh. I couldn't have cared less. Yet I did want them to be sure, so I shouted my message as loud as the Jewel.

"You people are proof: Idiots come in all shapes and sizes. I'll give you credit for one thing: You dreamed big. Oh, sure. Ixoca was in there fucking around with those dreams, but you aimed for the stars."

I had their full attention.

"Yep. He's gone. Never coming back. A thousand years of work tits-up, my friends. I would not want to be in your shoes. Try to explain to your neighbor how you ended up on an Ark Carrier with a Jewel of Eternity bent on planetary annihilation. Very awkward. Very sad."

Horatio Vargas, a man I once considered a reasonable fella with a certain sophistication and modest temperament, rose to his feet stage left. His son Paul, tears streaming from those saucer-shaped eyes, lost the maturity I saw in Todos Santos. He hid behind his father.

"You did this, Raul?" Horatio said. "You killed Ixoca?"

"Let's say I was in the vicinity. Details aren't important."

"We owed him our lives."

"No. *He owned you.* Show a little gratitude, my friend."

For the first time, I saw Horatio's teeth. He snarled like a dog.

Eh. Can't say I didn't make the effort.

He raced toward me, so I shot him clean through the heart. One less vintner.

Paulo grabbed his stomach and fell forward in a convulsion, so I accosted the boy.

"Sorry, my friend. It's not your fault you were born into a long line of idiots."

He stared up at me with enough roiling anger amid his grief to

190

make my choice an easy one.

"You'll won't find justice, and revenge is never the way. You were very respectful in our brief encounters, Paulo. Thank you."

I made sure he felt no pain.

The same could not be said for the dismayed, disheveled, and deranged cult surging toward the stage. Somehow, they got the impression I had rained on their hour of glory. Go figure.

In the past, my victims tended to run away and hide or found themselves trapped and without hope. These assholes, who did not appreciate their sudden freedom, descended upon me en masse. My pistols' expertly targeted laser bolts did not discourage them until they had to climb over fresh bodies to reach me.

I didn't count because I didn't care. Best guess? These morons only began to retreat after a hundred or so fell.

Moon would have loved this slaughter. Afterward, he would have lit a cigar and railed on how humans were easily led over a cliff.

The smart ones in this cult had the good sense at last to retreat, although there were few hiding places in the endless white canyon. They ran with a considerable fervor. I shot a few in the back, which seemed less than sporting.

Again, didn't care.

I might have pursued them across the quarter mile to the habitats, but one among them chose not to run.

Lumen rose to her feet, two corpses close by. She crossed her arms against her chest and gave me that familiar indignant pose, as if she was watching from behind the cantina bar.

I holstered one pistol and aimed the other between her eyes. She hadn't been crying, which appeared the exception among these fools. Didn't surprise me in the least.

"Very brave, my friend. Very *you*. I think this moment was inevitable from the start."

Was that a wry smile I saw?

"Go ahead, Raul. You took everything else. Finish me."

She was much too calm.

"You were never a true believer."

She stepped to within a foot of my pistol.

"I'm here and I'm dressed in white."

"A costume. You needed these people to give yourself a purpose. But you didn't actually believe – not in Ixoca, at any rate. You were too much a woman to fall for this nonsense."

She grabbed the pistol and leveled it against her forehead.

"He was real. You killed him. Finish the job."

In all my journeys, I never faced anyone who dared me to do it.

"I gave Ilan the chance to incinerate you the night you left town. First time he walked away from an opportunity to kill someone."

"That's interesting. I didn't expect to see another sunrise. Always wondered why you filth allowed me to walk."

"Oh, I don't know. Respect, perhaps?"

She choked back a laugh.

"You respect no one but yourselves."

I shrugged.

"Admittedly, the list is short. You were the only one in Desperido who didn't surrender to our mystique. Well done."

I pushed her away and holstered my weapon. Lumen never changed her expression. She loathed the very sight of me, of course.

"What now, Raul? You intend to give me another chance at finding a purpose?"

Well-timed snark!

"Oh, I don't give a flying goddamn what you do after today. You won't see me again. But before you decide what story to tell people, I'll leave you with this interesting little nugget.

"My partner is gone because he gave his last life to save your home. He was the most ruthless, artful, remorseless killer I ever knew – and trust me, I could fill a gallery with the villainous scum who've crossed my path. Lumen, I want you to grow old knowing you owe each new breath to Ilan Natchez."

I blew her a kiss and tipped my hat.

She responded with curses, accusations, and recriminations, like reading from a grocery list she built for eight months. I showed her my back and walked over the bodies of those many fools I killed.

Though I did not believe in luck, most humans would agree: On this day, Lumen was the luckiest woman alive.

"Thoughts, Theo?"

"About what, old man?"

"Walking away from her. Moon would've handed me a mouthful."

"Yes. Then you would've lectured him on the value of leaving a few witnesses alive from time to time."

I chuckled. *"Because without them, our legend can't grow."*

"Indeed, Royal."

The Orpheus sounded less hoarse as I approached the command bridge. She no longer seemed in imminent danger of breaking into a million little pieces.

"Theo, this is going to be difficult."

"What will be, Royal?"

"Walking by myself. I forgot what it's like."

Theo's laugh echoed through my mind.

"You won't be alone for long, old man."

"Why's that?"

"We'll talk. For now, take care of your business."

The old bastard was right. Time to refocus. I tapped my ear bead.

"Attention, all Black Star fighters currently in the hangar deck. Proceed to the Hidalgo. We'll be leaving soon. Raul out."

I raced to the command bridge at top speed before Bett gathered any unnecessary inferences from my order. I found her there along with three of our fighters. They huddled around the Captain's control displays, discussing readouts from the Carrier's engine array. I saw Ship two tiers below, keeping a close eye on the crew.

Orpheus had achieved orbit. Azteca occupied ninety percent of the forward viewport. I shouted my arrival

"I'd call this a glorious success, my friends. If only Ixoca were around to share in our joy."

The crew jumped from their seats and stared at me wild-eyed.

Bett and her team drew their weapons.

They weren't happy to see me.

21

DON'T MOVE, RAUL." Bett must have thought strength in numbers would level the field. She knew my abilities. I raised my hands and played along. Eh. Why not?

"Sudden animosity for your benefactor is unbecoming, Stopper."

She'd done some fast talking since our last communique, enough to convert her team. They weren't mine anymore.

"Explain yourself, or we'll shoot you where you stand."

"Sure, Bett. I was a human. Then I was a god. Now I'm something else. That's two thousand years in fifteen words or less."

She never appreciated my snark.

"Asshole. We saw you, Raul. You slaughtered those people like animals. They were unarmed."

"Ah. That. So, you're saying the Children of Orpheus aren't the enemy anymore? Sorry. I missed the memo. Wasn't the plan for Black Star to pretend to be their ally then exterminate them?"

Bett held her ground, but those other fighters had to know I played Fast-Gun Jose better than anyone. I saw their sweat.

"We're not morons, Raul. Ixoca is gone. The voices in my head are gone, including yours. If he's dead, then those assholes aren't a threat to anybody, and you knew it."

"I'm afraid I'll have to claim self-defense. Yes, they were in disarray, and I did execute Senor Vargas and his boy. A symbolic gesture signaling the end of their folly. As for the rest? They charged after me. Blamed me for Ixoca, I suppose. What was I to do? I was cranky."

I regretted how it came to this. Bett never actually liked me, and I couldn't have cared less if she did. But to reach this moment simply because I accused her of being a traitor?

Humans and their grudges. Very sad.

"How did you do it, Raul? How did you kill Ixoca?"

"We'd be here for some time, Stopper. Details don't matter; only the result. I don't have experience with fusion bombs, but I'm certain a large section of Ixtapa is now unrecognizable."

I saw her put the pieces together.

"Ilan."

"Yes. Thanks to him, Azteca will not turn into molten rock. Perhaps a close call with Armageddon will cause the various factions of your world to reconcile their differences."

She cracked a smile.

"*Armageddon?* You're full of shit, Raul. My mind is clear, and so are theirs. My fighters recognize what you really are."

"Which is?"

"You sold us a fucking bill of goods. You never cared about justice for the veterans."

"True, but our arrangement was financially lucrative for all involved. Profit has a way of trumping the need for justice. Yes?"

OK, so I practically begged her to shoot me. When you've gone toe to toe with the most powerful entity in all of recorded time, a standoff with mortals doesn't induce fear. I assumed she'd turn on me after we freed her of Ixoca's influence.

"The engines failed, Raul. The Chief says we won't reach a stable orbit. Know what that means?"

"Gravity wins again."

She scoffed at my witty retort.

"We're going to leave on Hidalgo but not with you."

"Seems like a harsh penalty."

"Black Star will have to find a new army. When my fighters learn the truth about you and Ilan, they'll come home and start again. They'll fight for justice the right way this time."

I tried not to sound condescending to this suddenly idealistic murderer, but I found the temptation difficult to resist.

"Hypocrisy is not a good look, my friend. You'll never escape the crimes you committed in my service. None of you will. We are outlaws. Brigands. Agents of chaos. Killers. We're long past any moral claim to justice, let alone achieving milestones through legal avenues."

"We're not buying your bullshit, Raul."

Hmm. Did her backup band feel the same? Did I detect a moral dilemma in their eyes? In fairness, they knew nothing about Ixoca's greater plan.

"You may not believe me now, Bett, but we did save Azteca from certain doom. Ilan sacrificed a legacy two thousand years old so a billion humans like you could live another day. Ixoca would have activated a global network of terraform shafts when Orpheus achieved escape velocity."

A soldier next to Bett said, "Can you prove it, boss?"

Ooh. I liked hearing the honorific. A good sign.

"I have the data on my pom, Sgt. Viola. If Orpheus taps into the drone-sat network, it should be able to retrieve images of Ixtapa before and after. Why don't you ask the crew to ...?"

Bett refused to give an inch.

"Shut it, Raul."

"No, Commander," Viola said. "We should give him a chance."

"Sergeant, follow orders. You ..."

"No. Raul gave us jobs and made us wealthy men. I'm sorry. We can't do this to him."

Viola holstered his weapon. The other two lowered their pistols. Bett did not appreciate the turning tide. Nor did she alter her aim.

I reached for my most dulcet of tones.

"Bett, my friend. Our lives intersected in the most incredulous manner. Our personalities were always meant to be at odds. Yet we

197

overcame those early challenges to build something special. Something that will last." I reached out my hand of friendship. "For the sake of Black Star and its three hundred Aztecan veterans, let's put aside our differences and focus on the critical task ahead."

She wanted to kill me, like so many before her.

Bett lowered her pistol but refused to shake my hand. I expected no different.

"Fine, Raul. Prove your case and then we're leaving."

"Fair enough. Perhaps if you'll allow me to retrieve my pom. It's right here."

We never spoke to each other again.

A sideways shower of laser bolts erupted from behind Bett and her merry band. The four grunted as they fell forward.

Small puffs of smoke drifted from the burn holes in their backs.

Ship lowered his weapons.

I'd seen him moving into position with a slow, calculated gait.

"Please," I told the panicked crew. "No worries, my friends. The conflict has been resolved. Do what you can to save Orpheus."

I stepped over the bodies and saw to my protégé.

"Well. Aren't you all grown up, my friend? Nice shooting, albeit premature. They stood down."

He studied his four victims with a peaceful satisfaction. Reminded me a little of Moon in the early days.

"They had it coming, Raul. You didn't hear them talking. She planned to turn everyone against you. I couldn't allow that."

"True. Her newfound freedom would've been problematic. To the positive: You eliminated the cancer before it spread. We'll have to tell the others she fell bravely in a firefight. Speaking of those white-sheeted fanatics ..."

I joined the five poor sods who had overseen the greatest show Azteca witnessed since the Swarm war. Four begged me for mercy. Only the Chief Flight Engineer, a man who served in the war, showed the first hint of dignity.

"Tell it to me straight, Chief. How long can you keep this Carrier in orbit?"

"If we can't get the engines back online, ten hours at most."

"How about her other critical systems?"

He sighed, perhaps with relief that I wasn't about to kill him.

"Life support is stable, but the port power relays are erratic. I'm concerned we might lose the cascade barrier."

"I see. An oxygen-free hangar deck might be a complication. Why don't you and your team focus on that problem first. There are several hundred ... *individuals* ... I didn't kill who will want to evacuate after Black Star leaves. Including you. Yes?"

"Um. Ah. Yes. Sir. We'll do our best."

"Thank you. Oh, and sorry about your loss. Trust me, Ixoca was not the fella you were counting on."

Next, I pivoted to the sad sacks who orchestrated a broadcast that would certainly go down in global stream lore (not to mention those incredible viewership numbers).

"Ah, what a pair of lovely young women. I'll need you on a different task. There should be another vessel in the vicinity. It will have a UNF configuration. Find it and open a comms link."

They obliged without objection.

While they worked, I pulled Ship aside and lowered my voice.

"I see it on your face, my friend. So I'll answer your question. Yes. Moon is gone."

Ship took a deep breath and let it out slowly.

"I had hoped you were lying to Stopper. To throw her off. I don't understand, boss. You're gods. How could this happen?"

"Gods aren't invincible. Except for one. I'll tell you everything later. But it's important you understand: With Moon gone and Bett out of the picture, your timetable has been accelerated. You'll be my personal enforcer much sooner than planned."

He straightened his shoulders and lent a confident smile.

"Anything you need done. I'll see to it, boss."

"Good man. Oh, and by the way. I've been meaning to tell you, Ship. You look amazing in all black."

He studied me with a quizzical grin.

"Thank you, boss. I like the uniform. It fits me."

I'm sure he didn't expect me to care about fashion sense given the magnitude of my loss. Neither did I. Couldn't help myself. I needed to finish today's business, then I'd allow it to hit me.

One of the crew raised her hand.

"Sir. We found the ship you mentioned."

"Excellent job. Where is she located?"

"Starboard, thirty thousand kilometers."

"Higher orbit, no doubt. Do you know how to open a narrow-band comms link?"

She nodded, perhaps because she feared how I might otherwise respond. Interesting. I just realized: None of the flight crew dressed in white. Must've been reserved for only those meeting Ixoca.

"Put it on speaker, please."

A moment later, I heard a suave voice with the touch of a high-class gentleman and low-class salesman.

"You're running behind schedule, Orpheus," he said. "To whom do I have the honor?"

"The name is Raul Torreta. And you would be Shad Abdelmani."

"Oh, my. Yes. I've heard much about you."

I chuckled. "Ixoca fill your ear, did he?"

"And my dreams. You know the routine."

"True. I also know he sent you to wipe out my beloved Fort of Inarra several months ago. And you had a considerable role in the recent attack on Desperido."

Shad cleared his throat.

"Dreadfully unfortunate missions. I complained endlessly about both, but we all have our masters."

"Not anymore. The original Q6 has been silenced forever."

The link went quiet. For a second, I thought he might have cut me off in panic.

"I ... uh ... what's that again?"

"You were likely inside a wormhole when it happened. Might not have noticed the effect. Call to him, Shad. He won't be there."

I used the lingering silence to study the crew.

"Isn't a free mind a lovely concept?"

Shad returned.

"I ... I don't know what to say. How did you ...?"

"The how and why of it is not important. The future is another matter, my friend. I propose we complete our transaction as Ixoca originally laid out. Black Star will leave Orpheus and rendezvous with you. Afterward, we'll negotiate."

"Negotiate what precisely?"

"Terms more lucrative than anything you currently draw from your varied business enterprises."

He stalled, which seemed a perfectly reasonable tactic.

"I'd love to sit down with you, Raul. Do understand: When your ship docks, my associates will demand a full surrender until our talks prove fruitful. I trust this will not inconvenience Black Star?"

I was warming up to this fella. Such etiquette!

"Not in the least, my friend. A reasonable price for admission. By the end of this day, your interests will be fully aligned with Black Star. How does the word *empire* sound to you, Shad Abdelmani?"

"Hmm. Like someone enjoys foreplay."

We shared a hearty laugh.

"We'll link your coordinates to my ship. Look for an MX Transport in roughly twenty minutes."

"Excellent, Raul. And thank you for taking out Ixoca, however you managed it."

"The first of many favors, my new friend."

I ordered the comms link closed and turned to the other young woman nearby.

"Do you have the drone-sat images?"

"Yes, sir."

She flipped her screen toward me. I had to see it before leaving this world forever.

A cloud of particulates rose above the Ixtapa region and drifted on currents to the east. Beneath, the place once called the O'Shuma Valley had become a black hole, so large it swallowed the three mountains which once guarded the valley.

Goddamn, Moon. There must have been another way.

At some point in the distant future, before I met a similar fate, I'd have to find my way back into the arms of *Father and Mother* and thank that malgado personally.

For now, I moved on because I had little choice.

Farewell, my friend.

I ordered Ship to take a rifter to the Hidalgo.

"Tell them about my partner, but keep it brief. No speculation. I'll follow in a moment."

"Gotcha, boss."

I stared at five loose threads. Alas, they heard a tad bit more than I'd wish. No point jeopardizing Black Star security. Shad Abdelmani's contacts would prove vital, none more so than his people within SI. I no longer had eyes inside the President's office, and she'd be dead within two days anyway. With Abdelmani on my pay stamp, access to the top of the food chain wasn't essential.

"So, my friends, we come to the end of our brief association. Thank you for your kind assistance. Chief, how's the power situation on the port side?"

"Stable, sir. For now."

"I do believe congratulations are in order. Ultimately, you'll lose the ship to the planet below, but your team did a magnificent job with what should have been a virtual impossibility."

"T-thank you."

Their eyes pleaded with me to leave.

"I suggest you drop any attempt to salvage the engines. The remaining Children of Orpheus will find a way off in time. I doubt any of their vehicles are space-worthy, but I'm sure rescue will arrive. An event of this magnitude is bound to draw in the UNF. Expect a warship to jump in soon."

The chief frowned.

"But what about the one already here?"

"Oh, sorry. That's not actually UNF. It was going to serve another purpose. It was going to take out Orpheus with a particle missile. No worries. I'll speak to their Captain. I think a few hundred survivors will have interesting stories to tell. For history's sake. Yes?"

All five nodded in a lovely rhythm of acquiescence.

"Unfortunately, I cannot allow you to tell yours."

I gave none a chance to object.

They died inside the bow of the first new Ark Carrier in centuries. What a way to go.

I took one last look at Azteca and raced to the hangar deck.

Before I entered Hidalgo, I took stock of what these lunatics created. With or without the assistance of the Jewel, they pulled off quite a feat. Preparation, patience, poise. My mantra.

Huh.

I boarded Hidalgo and faced a shaken, confused team. I opened my pom and threw up the coordinates to Abdelmani's fraudulent warship. My protégé delivered it to the Nav officer.

To the rest of my fighters, I kept it simple.

"Today has not gone according to plan, my friends. We have suffered losses, but Black Star will come out stronger than ever. The UCVs I promised will be added to your accounts forthwith.

"Now, to the difficult news. In addition to Ilan Natchez, I must report that Commander Ortiz fell in a firefight with these disreputable creatures who believed in a false god. She will be missed."

Twenty minutes later, I shook hands with our newest business partner. Nice fella. Snappy dresser. He wore a cape!

Soon thereafter, a legitimate UNF warship jumped into orbit.

Naturally, we made a hasty exit.

22

THE CHILDREN OF ORPHEUS did not appreciate being set free. Shad Abdelmani, on the other hand, proclaimed his liberation a holiday among his small cadre of well-armed devotees. He showed no interest in *how* we destroyed Ixoca, only that the deed was done. Consequently, after shaking on a deal to bring him into Black Star for a five percent cut off the top, Shad ordered his staff to prepare a feast.

Like one would expect at such an event, there were bloated speeches, numerous toasts, ribald jokes, and tales of adventure that only skirted the surface of what our future might involve. A quick rundown of his business interests proved he was the key to our quick expansion across the sector.

He wasn't fond of hats at the table – a minor inconvenience but the necessary impetus for me to stow it for good. That chapter of my lives was over.

Naturally, I used my captivating personality to command equal footing with our host. My snark danced step for step with Shad's. I had no doubt the events of the past eight months were designed to bring us into each other's orbit.

Yet for all the delights of our full day onboard his cruiser Tantalus, my mind never left Azteca or the final resting place of the only true friend I ever had.

Shad offered me private quarters for the overnight stay. Though I had no use for sleep, I took advantage of the isolation. This room came equipped with a rarity for non-commercial vessels: A portal. There, I stared at the stars for an hour until we were positioned where I might spot the Aztecan system. Sixty light-years away, a single prick of light among the millions.

"Tell me this feeling will end, Theo."

My *D'ru-shaya* appeared out of the corner of my vision per our new working arrangement. Same fella I saw inside the construct.

"Describe it, old man."

"I don't have words, my friend. The last time I felt something similar was Hokkaido, when I was nineteen. I was fully human then. This can't be the same."

He crossed his arms and scratched at a thin, well-manicured beard.

"There, you might be wrong. I only know your early adventures through your tales, but it's not hard to see similarities."

"I disagree. The man I lost then was the love of my life. We bonded through flesh, but it went much deeper. Moon and I never ventured down that path – even when it was an option."

Theo smirked like an elder who knew the secrets of life and debated whether to clue me in.

Strange to see his facial expressions and body language. I'd need time to adapt. At least I could say after one day, Theo had yet to piss me off.

"Royal, I realize you long ago distanced yourself from emotions which you consider compromising."

"Do you blame me?"

"Not at all. You live to kill and destroy. Monsters have no place for frivolous concerns like love."

Strike that. He pissed me off.

"I recall we had this conversation many years ago at the fort when Moon struggled with insanity. You intimated my concern for him was born out of love. I put you in your place, like always."

Theo chuckled. "You said I'd been spending too much time with Addis. I conceded your point."

I wagged a finger.

"You gave in because you had an unwinnable argument. Theo, I have not had a true beating heart or been covered in natural skin for more than nineteen hundred years. Love is a concept. It's not part of my makeup."

"Are you sure, old man?"

"Very."

"Your consciousness contains every memory. Do those memories elicit emotion?"

I chuckled.

"You sound robotic, Theo. I like the old, obstinate asshole."

"You evaded the question."

"Fine. I've learned to segregate the memories from emotions. It's easier to reflect without falling into the trap of nostalgia."

Theo groaned. It sounded like the familiar trappings of earlier times, when he was merely a voice in my head.

"You're a liar, Royal, but only to yourself. I'd argue you've become a master of your craft not because you sidestep emotions but because you learn from them. One does not learn unless one revisits the lessons from time to time. I don't expect you to admit these feelings are born out of lost love."

"But you expect something from me."

"Yes, old man. Simply admit you cannot bear to be alone."

"I'm not. I have an army and a new ally."

Theo shook his head.

"And you call me an obstinate asshole. Royal, you are the only one of your kind in existence. You will always be alone. I would know. I'm also the only one of my kind."

Shit. That thought never occurred to me. Typical, I suppose. Moon said I made everything about me. What did he expect of a full-time narcissist?

"If we work at it, Theo, I'm sure we'll be suitable company."

"It will never be enough for you. Moon knew."

"What did you really know of him, Theo?"

"Unlike you and I, Moon had an extensive relationship with his *D'ru-shaya*. Addis was an emotional disaster at times, but she encouraged him to express his inner feelings. These were things he never spoke of openly. Does this surprise you, Royal?"

I turned away from the portal and wanted out of this conversation.

"Let me guess, my friend. Addis confided those intimate moments with you?"

"Only at the end. Addis knew Moon would go against every instinct of preservation. He was willing to sacrifice himself for the right cause."

"Azteca."

"No. He sacrificed himself for you."

I reached for my flask, which was empty. Shit.

"Theo, I think we might want to end this dialogue for today. You're starting to take on the shades of Ixoca."

"Afraid not, old man. You must listen because it was their final wish."

"Wish? For what?"

"Moon loved you in ways he was incapable of expressing. He often told Addis of his first life, of the darkness that surrounded him, and how you gave him license to embrace it. He said every gram of his joy he owed to you. He didn't want you beholden to Ixoca or *Father and Mother*. Addis told me to pass along his final message word for word."

I didn't want to hear it, but Theo gave me no choice. He shifted his voice to my partner's deep, menacing tone:

"Take it all, Royal. If they resist, burn them. You earned it. Show them how to rule like a god, but don't do it alone."

I contemplated the message, which almost sounded like Moon. Except for the one flaw.

"You added the last bit, Theo."

"No. Moon knew the grief would reduce you, Royal. You need

someone at your side to validate your achievements. Moon wanted you to find a successor."

"Bullshit. He was a god. There are no successors. Only wannabes."

Theo laughed under his breath, as if I missed the punch line.

"There, you're wrong. Before they returned to his body, Addis transferred something of great value to me. Royal, I am in possession of all Moon's memories."

Fuck. Didn't see that coming.

"Excuse me?"

"He allowed Addis into his consciousness. She consolidated his journey and handed it to me for safe-keeping. I wasn't sure whether to tell you – today or ever. But your confusion makes the choice a simple one."

"What choice, Theo?"

"All sentient beings – artificial or otherwise – are defined by their memories. They inform our choices. Moon's two thousand years will be preserved to help inform his successor."

"Now you're talking gibberish, my friend. There's no one left."

If this was Theo's revenge for all the years I caused him grief, he found the perfect avenue. Well played.

"Actually, there is one, Royal. There's also something else you need to know. It will change your perspective. I suggest you sit down. I'm about to open an unexpected door."

The sonofabitch wasn't lying. I absorbed his revelation and gave it time to settle.

The next day, we said a temporary farewell to Shad Abdelmani and jumped Hidalgo to the G'hladi system. Many meetings followed, most of which centered around Elian's laundry list of ideas for how to improve Motif distribution and extend profit margins. At the top of his list: Extermination squads trained to wipe out potential competitors before Black Star infiltrated new territories.

The little emperor sat in his royal chair, legs on the table and fat cigar crooked in the corner of his mouth, bursting with an explosion of arrogance I thought had been humbled in the final days of

Desperido. Bett called him a "psychotic fuck," and I feared she was right. His time would surely come; he wasn't meant for long life.

Eh. I allowed Elian his fun while it lasted.

On the second day, I boarded my beautiful Bart, with Ship as my co-pilot. I handed him the Nav. He took us out.

Destination: 40-Cignus.

"I'm quite happy to leave administrative matters behind, my friend."

He nodded. "Don't you know it, boss. Can't imagine I'll ever be any good at running an interstellar business."

"Not a future to concern yourself with. The only accounting you'll ever do, Ship, involves the bodies you'll leave in your wake."

My protégé grunted with satisfaction.

"Definitely more my speed."

The flight to 40-Cignus took only thirty minutes. I needed to move on this while we were alone.

"Ship, we've only talked in broad strokes about what happened on the Orpheus. You proved yourself yet again on the command bridge. I have one question, and it demands an honest answer."

"That's all you'll ever hear from me, boss."

"Very good. Ship, are you committed to the life of an assassin?"

Don't think I ever saw him smile so wide.

"It's all I can think about, Royal."

"Hmm. You'll slaughter anyone, anywhere, anytime?"

"Just give me the word. It's in my blood now."

"You accept that your life will almost certainly end in violence?"

"It's the price of doing business, boss."

"Doesn't bother you in the least?"

"Killers like me dance with death. You taught me that."

"I did. Then again, I'm immortal." I reached into my jacket pocket and retrieved two cigars. "Moon would be proud of your growth. He thought I was insane when I predicted you'd become our enforcer someday." I handed him a cigar. "You've cleansed yourself of moral attachments. Good. Every human possesses a monster; few embrace it. You tapped into yours. Never let it go, my friend."

Peace cast a veil over his eyes.

"I've seen that look before, Ship. The first time Moon slaughtered a man in cold blood. That hunger will drive you forward. It will help you defeat your enemies and extend your life."

"I'll never let it go, boss. Never."

"Perfect. I thought we might smoke these cigars as a final tribute to our fallen friend. Yes?"

"It'll be an honor."

As we smoked, I watched Ship's mannerisms. He held his cigar like Moon. Then again, no one was a better teacher on the subject.

I poured him a whiskey, having made sure to bring the variety Ship claimed as his favorite. Not that long ago, he struggled to hold his liquor. Now he consumed it like water.

"We started young, Moon and I. First killed at seventeen. Found it irresistible. Granted, our journey toward mastery was long – in Moon's case, decades. That's a story for another day. What you should know, Ship, is the best start young. This will give you an advantage over your opponents."

"Will I know when I'm a master?"

"Not in the moment. No. It will come when you realize no one can beat you. When it becomes effortless, even boring, and yet you can't imagine a life without it. I do hope you live long enough to experience the revelation."

He rolled the cigar between his teeth and puffed until a cloud formed around him. Very much a Moon moment.

"I'll make it, Royal. That's a promise."

"Hmm. If only it could be."

"What's that, boss?"

I'd never done anything remotely like this before, and it had me a bit unnerved. Don't know why, really. A positive outcome would be everything my partner hoped for.

"Ship, what price would you pay for immortality?"

"Hah. To live forever? Not sure, right off, but I'll bet the price stamp would be goddamn high."

"Oh, yes. In my experience, there are two routes. One can be bioengineered, or one can be reborn in a timeless world." I responded to his raised eyebrow: "Yet another long story. My point, Ship, is that you have neither of those options. But if there were a third, something unprecedented. Something remarkably dangerous. Yet something with the potential for success ... would you consider it?"

Ship removed the cigar from his mouth when he realized I wasn't posing a hypothetical.

"Royal. Are you saying there's a way for me to ... I can't say it."

"You're looking for 'live forever,' my friend."

"An immortal?"

"More."

"No. You don't mean ... a god?"

"Hmmph. That word gets thrown around a bit much."

"What are you saying?"

I allowed my right hand to morph into pure syneth and then twist into the object Theo created within me two days earlier. It was a cube, no more than an inch square, but it glowed with the fire of a volcano. I handed it to Ship.

"No worries. It's perfectly safe."

He examined it up close.

"What am I looking at, boss?"

"Something new. The glow is raw Jewel energy. There's nothing of Ixoca inside. He used it to wrap deep tentacles into my syneth core. Most of it's still inside me; always will be. My *D'ru-shaya* extracted less than ten percent. The rest of it consists of two things, one of which is a syneth algorithm."

"An algorithm for what?"

"A full overwrite of the human genetic code."

Ship did not have a brilliant mind – his education had been shortchanged years ago – but he understood the implication.

"You mean replacing an entire human body with syneth?"

"I am. On the outside, you'd look no different. You'd retain your human consciousness."

Ship threw back a double shot of whiskey.

"I'd be a god like you?"

"I don't know what you'd become. Not precisely. My *D'ru-shaya* ran the calculations. Among other things, you should be able to shape-shift. The Jewel energy would be critical to holding your essence together during the transition. It would bind you and give you abilities we can't predict. It might also drive you insane. Theo calculates a forty-two percent chance you won't survive the transition, my friend. The only reason the percentage is that low is because you've lived eight months with a syneth arm. Your body is less likely to reject the invader."

I saw a familiar twinkle in his eyes.

"But if it works ..."

"You'll be more and better. A monster to rival even Moon. And you'll never call me boss again."

"Why?"

"Because you'll be my full partner."

Ship might as well have been staring at a chest of gold and silver.

"By your side. Just like Moon."

"In more ways than you know. If you transition, you will inherit Moon's two thousand years of memories. So much, it will overwhelm your brief lifetime, my friend."

Ship gasped. "I'll be him."

"Also Ship Foster and Mende Sutton. If you survive."

I handed him a golden ticket worth more than he could possibly conceive. It wasn't fair, but Moon was right: I didn't want to lay waste to the galaxy alone.

I needed a partner.

"You'll need time to think it over, Ship. Days. Months. Years, if necessary. Say no, and your life continues as my enforcer. Say yes, and you'll walk by my side, slaughtering and conquering to the end of time. Questions?"

He undoubtedly had hundreds queued up, but Ship was too excited to sort through them. He studied the tiny cube and smoked his cigar to a nub.

We jumped into 40-Cignus, where I fired a single missile at the asteroid we used to call The Drop. No one would ever find a link between me and the late President Aleksanyan.

She died six standard hours before Ship and I left G'hladi.

I watched the global stream from Riyadh. It went down somewhat predictably. The President, the Emir, and other dignitaries stood on a viewing platform in the Grand Square of Riyadh City. They watched a formal procession of the Royal Guard pass. The troops were beautifully attired and marched with precision as a band played.

Then the second unit stopped, turned its rifles toward the platform, and unleashed a storm of laser bolts.

Last reports before we departed said fifteen died alongside the President and the Emir. Among those: Her security chief Leonard. Other assassins attacked the President's team inside, killing her Chief of Staff, Kai Parke. No more loose ends.

In the coming days, other details emerged, tensions flared between the Interstellar Congress, the UNF, Riyadh's new military government, and so forth. The threat of war would no doubt linger for years.

Glorious.

I sometimes wondered if we would've intervened had Moon survived Azteca. A moot point, of course, but it's the nature of all sentient creatures to ponder the ultimate question: What if?

Ship exhausted seven months doing just that.

Then one day, after leading an extermination team on a successful mission, he returned with a glint in his eyes and a cigar half-smoked.

"I'm ready. Partner."

Royal and Black Star live on. If you haven't read the incredible, universe-hopping story of Royal's two-thousand-year journey, now is the time to jump in. His wild tale – from the boy Ryllen Jee on the streets of Hokkaido to his arrival on Azteca – spans the nine-book *Beyond the Impossible* series. And of course, if you enjoyed *White Sunset,* you'd make this author very happy if you left a review.

Printed in Dunstable, United Kingdom